CAPTIVE!

Lucy groped around the small room, which was a little larger than she was. Perhaps, she thought, Miss Brill had in mind to kill her. She could easily strangle Lucy in a flash and no one would know. She could put the children to bed, come down to the kitchen, strangle Lucy Forever, put her in a green garbage bag, and toss her in the trash can. There would be no evidence whatsoever.

Other Bullseye Books you will enjoy

Confessions of an Only Child by Norma Klein
The Kid in the Red Jacket by Barbara Park
The Secret Life of the Underwear Champ by Betty Miles
There's a Boy in the Girls' Bathroom by Louis Sachar
Witch Week by Diana Wynne Jones

DR. M. JERRY WEISS, Distinguished Service Professor of Communications at Jersey City State College, is the educational consultant for Bullseye Books. Currently Chair of the International Reading Association President's Advisory Committee on Intellectual Freedom, he travels frequently to give workshops on the use of trade books in schools.

Lucy Forever & Miss Rosetree, Shrinks

SUSAN SHREVE

Bullseye Books · Alfred A. Knopf
New York

A Bullseye Book
Published by Alfred A. Knopf, Inc.

Copyright © 1987 by Susan Shreve
Cover art copyright © 1988 by Doron Ben-Ami

Library of Congress Catalog Card Number: 86-29513
ISBN: 0-394-80570-4
RL: 5.3

Manufactured in the United States of America
  2 3 4 5 6 7 8 9

For Elizabeth

·1·

When Lucy Forever got home from school, very late as usual because of detention in language arts for daydreaming, Miss Rosetree was already in the office of Shrinks, Incorporated.

Lucy ran up the front steps of her house on Rugby Road, read the note on the hall table from her mother, and rushed to the cornflower blue bedroom—hardly changed at all since her mother had decorated it for the baby boy the doctor had assured her she was having when Lucy Forever was born.

She took off her school clothes, kicked them out of sight under the bed with yesterday's school clothes, two trashy books, and a half-eaten bowl of cornflakes swimming in sour milk.

Then she put on panty hose, an old bra of her mother's, which she stuffed with pale pink toilet paper, a serious-looking gray suit only slightly too large that had belonged to her grandmother, and black high-heeled sandals her mother had worn for formal occasions. In the mirror over her mother's dressing table, she brushed out her long, thin black hair and tied it in a tiny lopsided bun. She put on blush, black mascara with extra thickness, plum lipstick, and wire-rimmed glasses without the glass. Then she took a briefcase full of case studies from under the bed, went around the side of the house to the basement door, behind which the offices of Lucy Forever and Miss Rosetree, Shrinks, Incorporated, were located, and went in.

"Good afternoon, Miss Rosetree," Lucy Forever said, nodding to the young, soft-bodied blond girl dressed as a woman who was bent over a case study opened in front of her on the desk.

"I'm sorry to be so late. Any tragedies?"

"Not so far," Miss Rosetree said, not looking up.

Lucy Forever opened her briefcase full of manila folders on her own desk, found one particular folder marked "The Parks Divorce," and picked up the disconnected telephone. "One of my clients was going to jump from the roof of Friendly's ice cream store because his girlfriend was spending all of her time with a Siamese cat."

"Did he jump?" Miss Rosetree asked absently.

"Of course not. That type never jumps. He asked me to get him a double-dip chocolate mint ice cream cone while he thought about it. I wasted my whole morning." Lucy Forever sat down at her desk and took a pencil and note pad out of the center drawer. "Hello, Mrs. Parks," she said. "This is Dr. Forever of Shrinks, Incorporated. I'm calling about your divorce." She shook her head, rolling her eyes at Miss Rosetree. "I know he's a terrible man. I know he beats you on Fridays and makes you eat vegetables while he eats steaks for his anemia. I know he gave away your pet turtle to the zoo. Really, Mrs. Parks, I have no patience with you. Any woman who puts up with a man as miserable as Mr. Parks deserves to be given away to the zoo herself. Goodbye, Mrs. Parks. I suggest you find a new psychiatrist." She put down the telephone, closed the folder on the Parks divorce, and dumped it in the wastebasket. "Hello," she said, lifting the receiver, listening, then putting her hand over it. "It's Mrs. Parks again," she said to Miss Rosetree. "Yes, Mrs. Parks. I see. Let me look at my appointment book. If you can come right this minute I can see you, but you must hurry. I have a client coming at four o'clock who's a very serious case."

Lucy Forever looked stricken. She put her head against her fist and bit the eraser end of her pencil.

"So what's the matter with Mrs. Parks now?" Miss Rosetree asked.

"Well, it looks as though Mrs. Parks may come to a desperate end this very afternoon," Lucy said. "Mr. Parks came home from work in a bear costume and said he was going to eat her for dinner."

"Cooked or not?" Miss Rosetree asked without a trace of a smile.

"She didn't say."

The office of Shrinks, Incorporated, was located in the basement of Lucy Forever's house on Rugby Road in Charlottesville, Virginia, two blocks up from the University of Virginia. It had been a recreation room when the former owners lived there, but Lucy's father, who was British, did not believe in a great many things, including recreation rooms.

"Children grow moldy in basements," he had said when Lucy suggested moving the storage boxes and tools and mementos and unused furniture out of the basement and

· 3 ·

turning it into a recreation room as it was meant to be. Lucy Forever's father was a child psychiatrist trained in London who tended to be formal, even with his daughter, and chilly, according to her friends. He had converted the garage behind the house on Rugby Road into his office. His patients walked up the driveway, sometimes with their parents, sometimes alone, past the door of Shrinks, Incorporated, and along a flagstone path to the old garage, where Lucy's father sat hour after hour in a reclining leather chair, with a stenographic notebook in his lap, listening to the terrible lives of children.

One Saturday, uninvited, Lucy had looked through the notebooks on her father's desk and found page after page filled with incompetent drawings of Mickey Mouse and Petunia Pig and Elmer Fudd and hundreds of plump, two-feathered birds with open beaks.

"Are these the notes you keep on children?" Lucy asked when her father came into the office.

"Of course," he said crossly, "and they're highly confidential."

"But they're cartoons, Daddy."

Her father had turned the color of a bright red tomato.

"Perhaps," he said, making a great effort to control his temper, which Lucy could see was about to explode like a water balloon in the office, "you and your friend Rosie should start your own psychiatry practice and leave mine alone."

Rosie Treeman was Lucy Forever's best friend since nursery school at First Baptist, Main Street, when Lucy Childs became Lucy Forever—forever.

Lucy had arrived with her mother at the entrance to First Baptist Nursery on the first day of school, having made very clear that morning at breakfast that she wasn't going to school ever in her life and certainly not that particular Monday morning in September. At the door of First Baptist was a soft pancake of a girl, half Lucy's size, holding tight as death to her mother's hand with one hand and to the door with the other.

"I'm not going," the child said to her mother.

"Me neither," Lucy said, glad to have so quickly found an ally in enemy territory.

Far above her head, Lucy's mother talked in whispers to the mother of the other child. Then she bent down, took Lucy's face in her hands and said, "Please, Lucy, this little girl named Rose is very frightened about going to school this morning. Won't you help her out?"

And Rosie's mother bent down, took her daughter's face in her hands and said, "Please, Rose, this little girl named Lucy is very frightened about going to school this morning. Won't you help her out?"

So in a matter of seconds Lucy was holding tight to Rosie's plump hand, and their mothers had flown out of the room, into the world, away from them.

When the teacher, whom Lucy remembered now mainly as smelling of onions and sweet perfume, called Lucy's name, she said she couldn't read her last name on the roll book.

"What is your name?" she asked Lucy.

"Lucy," she answered, gripping Rosie's hand as if it would evaporate.

"I mean your last name," the teacher said.

"I'm Lucy Forever," she replied in a voice so tiny she didn't recognize it as her own.

"Forever." The teacher laughed merrily. Some of the children in the circle began to laugh. A little boy next to her in Oshkosh overalls with a hole in the knee bopped Lucy on the shoulder.

"There's no such name," he said.

"What is your real last name?" the teacher asked through her laughter, which fell like rainwater over the children. "I know it can't be Forever."

Lucy was too stricken to remember her real last name.

"Her name is so Lucy Forever," Rosie said in a tiger-sized voice. "I met her mother right there," she pointed to the door where the mothers had been standing. "And I asked 'What's your name?' and she said to me 'Mrs. Forever.' "

And that was that.

On the playground that morning, Lucy sat next to Rosie in the wet sand of the sandbox and said, "You will be my best friend."

"Forever," Rosie had replied earnestly.

So they had been through First Baptist into Haddenfield Elementary School, where Lucy was now in one sixth-grade class and Rosie was in the other.

Since nursery school, they had been in partnership. First they had a grocery store in Lucy's mother's studio until her mother discovered that they were selling real food and that a large family of mice was happily reproducing on the shelves. Then they were veterinarians taking care of sick stuffed animals—an occupation that lasted until Lucy gave a koala bear some baby aspirin and ate the rest of the bottle herself. By fourth grade Lucy wanted to be a rock-and-roll singer, so they started "Singers of the Dark of Night," playing rock music in the living room while Mrs. Childs sculpted in her studio and Dr. Childs listened to children in his office behind the house. They spent hours choreographing dance routines, doing leaps from the couch to the coffee table to the small French chairs in the living room, until Dr. Childs said enough was enough. Either the rock-and-roll group retired immediately, or he was going to move into his office for the rest of the year.

Walking home from school early in September of sixth grade, Lucy brought up the possibility of psychiatry with Rosie.

"How would you like to be a shrink?" she asked. At eleven, she towered above Rosie, pole-like with long legs and a torso so slender the shoulder bones protruded, forming inexact V's through her turtlenecks. She had, according to her mother, a pretty face, with high cheekbones and the high flush of an English girl's complexion, but she hid behind long straight hair too thin to wear long, which she refused to cut.

"I don't know about psychiatry," Rosie said. "I'd really rather be someone famous."

"We could be famous shrinks. The most famous women psychiatrists in America. Only the terrible cases will come to us."

Rosie considered the possibilities. "Like suicides?"

"Worse," Lucy said with great confidence. "Like men who think they're German shepherds. That sort of thing."

Rosie brightened. "Or a woman who falls in love with a zebra in the zoo and lives in the cage with him in the hopes of turning into a zebra herself. That could be quite a lot of fun," she said happily. Rosie looked much younger than

Lucy, with tight blond curls hugging her round head like a cap and soft flesh around her waist and hips—baby fat, her mother called it—that refused to leave. "But what will your father think?"

"Psychiatry was my father's idea. He sees it as a quiet afternoon activity," Lucy said.

"What if we are more famous than he is?"

"Then he'll just have to suffer," Lucy said, not for a minute imagining that famous was exactly what they would become.

That night at supper Lucy asked Dr. Childs once again about the recreation room, but this time as an office for Shrinks, Incorporated.

"You know how I feel about basements," he said in a faraway voice.

"Please, darling," Mrs. Childs pleaded. "It's a wonderful out-of-the-way idea."

"Besides," said Lucy, "I'd spend quite a lot of time outside. I'm planning to have all kinds of patients like zebras and German shepherds, which you can hardly expect to lie on a couch in the basement."

So Dr. Childs agreed reluctantly, in spite of his principles. He even went to the hardware store one Saturday to buy pale yellow paint for the large basement room. Mrs. Childs picked up a rug at a yard sale and donated the furniture that had been in Dr. Childs's old office at the University of Virginia Hospital before he went into private practice.

By November, Shrinks, Incorporated, was in full swing. According to the files kept in an old file cabinet, Miss Rosetree and Dr. Forever had four hundred and sixty-eight patients with serious mental disorders.

· · ·

On the afternoon that Mr. Parks came home in a bear costume with the intention of eating Mrs. Parks for supper, Miss Rosetree was working on her chart entitled "Samantha and the Zebra," a case in which, according to the most recent entry by Miss Rosetree, Samantha had begun to develop black stripes on her belly.

When Dr. Forever told her that Mrs. Parks was arriving shortly, Miss Rosetree closed the Samantha file, put it in the file drawer, went to the bathroom and changed into an old red taffeta gown that had belonged to Mrs. Childs. Then she ran up the basement steps, out the front door, around to the driveway, and down to the basement door, where the sign Shrinks, Incorporated, hung. It was done in red oil-base paint, with tiny rosebuds drawn on it by Mrs. Childs. She knocked.

"Come in," Lucy Forever said.

Miss Rosetree, as Mrs. Parks, rushed in, slammed the door, and fell over on the floor in a red taffeta heap.

"Mrs. Parks, you *must* pull yourself together or I'll have to call an ambulance and cart you away this afternoon."

"I can't pull myself together. I can tell he's going to eat me. He looks starved to death."

"Please lie down on the couch, Mrs. Parks."

Mrs. Parks pulled herself to her feet, limped over to an army cot covered with a gray blanket, and lay down, panting heavily.

"Now tell me, Mrs. Parks, how do you feel?"

"*Scared*."

"I bet you feel very scared."

"You're right I do. Terrified."

"What are you terrified of, Mrs. Parks?"

"*Bears*," said Mrs. Parks.

"Aha," Lucy Forever said, taking out a stenographic pad just like the one her father used. "Scared of bears. Now tell me, Mrs. Parks, what do you remember of bears in your childhood?"

Mrs. Parks began to cry. "I see a big black bear at Yellowstone Park. He is lumbering towards me with his huge pink mouth watering. I try to run and I can't move. 'Here beary—nice beary,' I say. 'Be good to Mrs. Parks.' "

"You weren't Mrs. Parks then."

"Shut up. I'm feeling things like you told me to."

"Go ahead."

"He comes right up to me so close I can feel his hot breath and see his bright red tonsils. Do bears have tonsils?"

"Of course," Lucy Forever said, exasperated. "And then what?"

Mrs. Parks shrieked.

"And then—oh no, it's too awful to tell."

Lucy Forever picked up the telephone. "Ambulance, please. Send an ambulance to 809 Rugby Road, Shrinks, Incorporated. I have a patient who just went crazy. And hurry. She's hurting my ears."

Mrs. Childs rushed down the back steps.

"My lord, what is going on, Lucy?"

Rosie stopped screaming and sat up on the army cot.

"Mrs. Parks just went crazy and I've had to call an ambulance," Lucy said.

"Did you honestly call an ambulance?" Mrs. Childs asked.

Lucy rolled her eyes. "What do you think I am, Mother? Crazy?"

"Yes, darling, that's exactly what I sometimes think you are." Mrs. Childs went back upstairs.

Rosie changed to her gray corduroys and I LOVE YOU RAIDERS red turtleneck, put the taffeta dress back in the trunk they used for dress-up, washed the peach makeup off her cheeks, and went back into the office.

"Shhh," Lucy said. She was sitting at her desk peering through her glassless glasses at the window just to the left of the door leading outside. Staring in the window was a tiny girl the color of pears with long, silky black hair and eyes shiny as polished silver—full of terror.

"Do you know her?" Rosie asked.

"I've never seen her. She must be a patient of my father's."

Rosie went to the door and opened it.

"Should we ask her to come in?"

"Maybe," Lucy said.

She went over to the little girl, who was dressed for a birthday party in a bright blue dress with lace and sequins and ribbons, and a large bow in the back. She knelt down so they were the same size.

"Hello," she said. "My name is Dr. Forever."

The child lifted both hands and covered her shiny eyes with the flats of her palms so she couldn't see Lucy. But she didn't try to leave. In fact, with her eyes still covered she took a step closer, so in the light of the sun setting just behind the roof of the Childs's garage, Lucy could see the beginnings of a bright red scar just above the collar of the child's fluffy dress.

· 2 ·

It was Rosie's idea to bring the child into the office of Shrinks, Incorporated. She sat her down in front of an old steamer trunk full of second-hand toys collected in the neighborhood by Lucy and kept for the make-believe children who came to the offices of Dr. Forever and Miss Rosetree.

"We have lots to play with," Rosie said, reaching into the trunk. "This one," she said, taking out a naked doll with a plastic head and blinking eyes and a cloth stomach leaking its stuffing, "is my favorite. She was left in an azalea bush in the middle of winter by her mother, and I found her there on a terrible snowy night."

The child had not taken her hands away from her eyes, but one plump finger moved just enough for Rosie to see the black center of a blue-green eye.

"The doll's name is Anna Maria Treeman," Rosie said. "She's eight months old and Catholic."

Very gently Rosie put Anna Maria on the child's lap. "She's sleeping, of course, but you can hold her if you like."

Lucy sat down on the floor next to Rosie, rummaged

through the trunk for clothes to put on poor Anna Maria, and found a ripped apple-green gingham, which she laid on the naked doll. "You can dress her," she said, but the child shook her head. "Tell the story about how you adopted this baby, Miss Rosetree."

Rosie settled against the trunk of toys. "Well, I was out in an awful storm inspecting the neighborhood for criminals, which I do every night. Just as I passed Dr. Forever's garden, I heard a strange cry like the cry of a kitten or a young raccoon coming from one of the huge azalea bushes. So I went over to the bush, carefully shined my flashlight into the center of the branches, and there, stark naked and howling, was Anna Maria, frightened almost to death. So I picked her up, took her home, put her in a warm bath because she was blue, and tucked her into my own bed. And the next morning the priest came over and baptized her a Catholic or my mother wouldn't have let her stay in the house."

"Then," Lucy said, lying on her stomach with her chin resting in her hands, "Miss Rosetree called the police and made a search for her mother, whom she found on the highway driving a meat truck, which was her job.

" 'I don't have time for a baby,' the truck-driver mother said. 'There's no place for a baby in a truck.' Miss Rosetree said she was sorry to hear that. 'Who's going to take care of her?' she asked. 'Beats me,' the truck driver said, 'unless you do. That's why I dropped her off in a nice neighborhood, thinking she'd have advantages.' So Miss Rosetree, who hasn't any children of her own, kept her, and she stays here for children like you who come to our office."

Slowly the child began to take her hands away from her face. But just at the moment the child dropped her hands and picked up the doll, a large-boned woman who looked in every way like a man, except she was wearing a white nurse's uniform and cape and cap, knocked on the door of Shrinks, Incorporated.

Lucy leapt to her feet and answered the door.

"Cinder," the nurse said, not sharply but certainly not with great warmth either.

The child stood up without turning around, still clutching Anna Maria. As Rosie reported later to Lucy Forever, who couldn't from her position at the door see the child's face, Cinder took one hand off the doll, reached up to the collar of her dress, and pulled, exposing the length of what appeared by its bright red color to be a very recent scar.

"Would you like to keep Anna Maria until you come back to see Dr. Childs?" Rosie asked.

Cinder didn't reply, but she wrapped her arms tightly around the doll, took the hand of the nurse, and walked out.

"She didn't talk to you, did she?" the nurse asked Lucy Forever.

"No," Lucy replied.

"I would imagine not," the nurse said, and Lucy watched them walk together up the flagstone path. At the street, the nurse took the child's shoulder as if she would lift her off the ground and led her across.

"So," Lucy said, packing up the rest of the toys, clearing her desk of case studies, and replacing them in her file cabinet. "What do you think?"

"I think someone probably slit her throat clear through to the voice box," Rosie said matter-of-factly.

"Brother, you have the bloodiest imagination I ever knew," Lucy said going up the basement steps.

Rosie followed Lucy to the kitchen, where they had milk and Oreos every afternoon after Shrinks, Incorporated, closed.

"What do you think?" Rosie asked.

"I think she could talk if she wanted to," Lucy said.

"What about her throat?" Rosie asked. "She showed me the scar. It's this long," she measured with her hands.

"Somebody certainly cut it," Lucy said, and if her mother had not at that very moment walked in from her studio, her hands wet with clay, Lucy would have given Rosie her own theory about Cinder's throat.

"Your mother wants you home for supper, Rosie," Mrs. Childs said, rinsing off her hands in the sink. "And you have a piano lesson, Lucy."

"I quit piano Tuesday," Lucy said, rinsing her glass and putting it in the dishwasher.

"So Mr. Van Dyke said, and I told him you weren't allowed to quit until your twelfth birthday, on principle."

"I have always hated principles. And piano," Lucy said crossly.

"On the subject of principles, I saw one of your father's patients come out of Shrinks, Incorporated, a little while ago. Which, as you know, is against your father's principles."

Rosie shot Lucy a quick glance of danger.

"I know," Lucy said. "She just wandered in. We couldn't very well say 'Split, beat it, leave us alone. You're not allowed in here on principle.' She might have been a manic-depressive and decided to commit suicide right there on the spot."

"I very much doubt it," Mrs. Childs said.

"Who knows?" Lucy said, going with Rosie to the front door. "Anything can happen."

"Just tell your father about her tonight at supper. He'd want to know," Mrs. Childs said, taking pork chops out of the refrigerator and then snapping off the heads of the dead daisies in a vase on the kitchen table.

"I hope you're not in trouble," Rosie whispered.

"Don't worry."

"I mean I hope now we won't have to quit Shrinks, Incorporated, like we had to quit 'Singers of the Dark of Night.' "

"Not a chance. My parents like Shrinks, Incorporated. It's quiet and clean and my father honestly believes we're playing an intellectual and character-building game. So goodbye, Miss Rosetree. See you in the office tomorrow at three if I don't have detention."

"Goodbye, Dr. Forever," Rosie said. She then ran home to a small frame house three blocks north, on the edge of a solidly Catholic neighborhood chock full of children and next door to the Church of the Immaculate Conception where she lived with her parents, four brothers, five sisters, her grandmother, her aunt, an old dachshund without any teeth, and ten goldfish, one for each child.

Dr. Anthony Childs was a well-known psychiatrist who had a reputation for helping children other psychiatrists had failed to help. People had come from all over the East Coast to attend his clinic at the University of Virginia Hospital, and when he left the hospital to open his own office on Rugby Road, parents still brought their children from as far away as Washington, D.C., especially if their problems were very serious.

"Your father is a genius with children," Mrs. Childs would say dreamily to Lucy while Dr. Childs was working. Lucy was certainly not one to argue that point, and she had almost always respected his rules without question—an attitude she seldom took toward other rules. These included: (1) never coming to the office during patient hours; (2) never answering the doctor's telephone in the house; and (3) never speaking to a patient who happened to pass by the house on the way to the office. In fact, Dr. Childs had once said shortly after he opened his office that Lucy should pretend his small patients were ghosts whom she couldn't even see in the light of day.

"Why don't they want to be seen?" Lucy had asked.

"Psychiatry is a private matter. People tell us their secrets, and sometimes they are ashamed to be seeing us at all. It's a matter of principle to respect their privacy."

So when Dr. Childs left his office the afternoon of Cinder's visit and walked up the gray flagstone path just as Lucy was leaving the house for her dreaded piano lesson, she told him about the child's visit to Shrinks, Incorporated. To her astonishment, he did not seem to be at all concerned.

"As long as she came to see you, my love, and you didn't bring her into your playroom or stop her on the path," he said in a faraway voice, which was always a warning to Lucy that he was lost in one of the awful secrets of a child. "Have a lovely piano lesson," he said vacantly.

"I hate piano," Lucy said. "You know I hate piano. I may as well be a canary for all anyone in this house knows about me," she snapped.

When she was halfway up the walk, her father called to her. "The little girl didn't talk to you, did she?"

"No, she didn't make a sound," Lucy said.

He shook his head. "I didn't think so," he said and went into the kitchen, where he kissed Mrs. Childs as usual as if he hadn't seen her for twelve years.

On the way to piano, a plan began to form in Lucy's mind. All through the lesson, she imagined what she and Miss Rosetree could do the next time Cinder visited Dr. Childs. She missed the chords on "O What a Beautiful Morning." She forgot the second flat when there were two flats on the score.

"*Pianissimo. Pianissimo,*" Mr. Van Dyke kept saying as if his ears would fall off his head while she was playing "Do, Lord."

At the end of the lesson, she explained to Mr. Van Dyke that although she loved piano very much, she would not be coming back to see him for the next few weeks because— and this was a confidence she hoped he wouldn't break— she had run into mental problems and was going to be seeing a psychiatrist at the very same hour as piano lessons.

"Your father?"

"Of course not my father," Lucy said. "He's not even supposed to know. He'd feel terrible to find out I'd turned mental living in the very same house with him," Lucy said. "I want you to promise not to tell my parents. They will think I'm here, of course. It would make them miserable to know I had a problem."

Mr. Van Dyke pulled his trousers up to the middle of his waist, buckled his belt tighter, and looked sadly at Lucy Forever.

"I'm very sorry to hear about your situation," he said, "but I don't know if I can lie to your parents."

"Mr. Van Dyke," Lucy said in a very low voice. "I remember when you told my mother I had talent, so I know you don't really mind telling lies."

A funny smile turned the corners of Mr. Van Dyke's lips.

"Anyway, I'll only miss about three lessons. I plan for this mental problem to be fixed by my twelfth birthday," Lucy said and left the house with a light heart. It had been easier than she had ever imagined. Mr. Ethan Van Dyke was soft as cottage cheese. With a little more persuasion, she probably could convince him to fly to Saturn if she wanted.

Lucy didn't even wait to get home before she called Rosie Treeman. In fact, she walked straight across Main Street from Mr. Van Dyke's to the pay phone outside the entrance of Daily's Drugs and dialed the number.

Rosie had gone straight home for supper, which was always early at the Treeman's house because Rosie's father worked construction and came home at five o'clock starved for dinner. After dinner the children did homework and chores, brushed their teeth, said their prayers, and went to bed. They slept three to a room except the baby, who slept in a crib in Mr. and Mrs. Treeman's room.

Rosie's job was dishes every night, which is what she was

doing just as Lucy called her from the pay phone on Main Street.

"Did you get in trouble about the little girl?" Rosie asked first off.

"My father says as long as patients come to us and we don't stop them or *make* them come in, then there's no problem of principles. I couldn't believe it."

"That's wonderful. I thought all the way home that Shrinks, Incorporated, was going to have to close tomorrow afternoon."

"Not at all. What I've been thinking is that we might expand just a little. Maybe Cinder will stop by next week on Tuesday when she comes to see my father. I've even canceled piano with soft-boiled Van Dyke so I won't have to leave the office early on Tuesdays, just in case Cinder starts to talk."

"You know, Dr. Forever," Rosie said with great excitement, "I was thinking the exact same thing." She finished the dishes, dried them, and put them away. Then she kissed her father, who was watching TV; her mother, who was changing the baby; and her grandmother, who was, as usual, reading the New Testament with a magnifying glass. Then she brushed her teeth, went to her own room, and while she thought of the mute child, said her prayers and climbed into bed. Her sister older by eleven months was reading *True Romance* in the lower bunk. Her sister younger by two years was doing her math. Rosie lay on her back, her eyes wide open, and imagined the possibilities of real patients instead of make-believe ones at Shrinks, Incorporated.

· · ·

Lucy's parents were just sitting down to dinner when Lucy arrived.

"So how was piano?"

"Wonderful."

"Wonderful?" Mrs. Childs looked confused. "You had a good lesson?"

"I had an awful lesson, of course, but I think Mr. Van Dyke is a prince."

Mrs. Childs gave Dr. Childs an odd look.

"There are all kinds of princes in the world, I suppose," Dr. Childs said. "So Lucy tells me one of my patients stopped by to see her today," Dr. Childs said, serving dinner.

"I'm glad she told you. I told her she ought to mention it," Mrs. Childs said, and she was just about to tell Dr. Childs what she did that day in her studio, as she always did at dinner, when Dr. Childs, who never talked about his patients on principle, at dinner or any other time, interrupted.

"Honest to God, if Lucy could get that child to talk, I'd give her a Rolls-Royce, a gold medal of honor, a house in the country."

"My own telephone?" Lucy asked quickly.

"I doubt that," Dr. Childs said.

"Why doesn't she talk?" Lucy asked, quickly realizing that her father would not answer her, that the subject of Cinder was closed.

But already Lucy was a week ahead, thinking about the little girl and how Dr. Forever and Miss Rosetree could persuade her to talk.

· 3 ·

Early on Saturday morning, Lucy Forever brought the portable color television, a box of multicolored Fruit Loops, and Bolivar, her brain-damaged cat, into her bedroom.

Rosie was busy. On Saturdays Rosie was always busy with choir practice and catechism and two hours plus of chores.

"Two hours plus," Mrs. Treeman said now that Rosie was in the sixth grade, and sometimes the plus went on and on until bedtime. But to Lucy's great surprise, Rosie called between choir practice and catechism, just as Lucy was settling into an hour of cartoons.

"You'll never guess what," Rosie said breathlessly into the pay phone at University and Main. She was trying to talk above the sound of the traffic. "What?" Lucy asked. Early that morning, Rosie had been on her way to St. Vincent's Roman Catholic Church when a long black car that looked very much like a hearse stopped at the light beside the University of Virginia Hospital. Rosie noticed the car immediately because it was a hearse, and she even looked in the back window for the casket, which was not there. However, the back wasn't empty. Peering out, with her nose pressed flat against the window, was the mute child Cinder, the first real patient in Shrinks, Incorporated's psychiatric career. "And then you'll never guess what," Rosie said. "In the driver's seat, looking like a stork without the feathers, was your awful piano teacher."

"Mr. Van Dyke?"

"Exactly," Rosie said, full of pleasure.

"And then what?"

Then, Rosie said, she had crossed the street and walked in back of the hearse very close to the window so the child could see her. Which she did, and covered her eyes with her hands and ducked behind the glass.

"I suppose you were wearing ordinary clothes," Lucy said disdainfully.

"I was wearing a skirt because I have to wear one to catechism."

"Oh brother," Lucy said. "Now she'll know you're not a real psychiatrist but just an ordinary child," Lucy said.

Rosie hesitated. "I think she knows that already, Dr. Forever."

Lucy turned off the television, poured a small pile of Fruit Loops on the bed for Bolivar, who ate only cereal and yogurt since an encounter three years earlier with a VW camper. The van had been traveling too fast on Rugby Road and had damaged the cat's small brain beyond repair. Now he curled happily on Lucy's lap and ate his Fruit Loops a few at a time with his paw.

Now that she knew the dreadful Mr. Van Dyke was involved with Cinder, she had to find out everything she possibly could about the mute child.

From downstairs, Mrs. Childs called, as she did almost every Saturday morning, to see if Lucy was interested in an afternoon drive in the Blue Ridge Mountains to see the wildflowers.

"Maybe," Lucy said, which meant "no" politely. She hated afternoon drives with her parents, especially in the Blue Ridge Mountains. She would sit in the back seat, mildly carsick, while they talked about wildflowers and the cost of flying to Europe and whether to have a dinner party in the spring or wait until summer. Usually Lucy daydreamed on these outings or read *Soap Opera Digest*, which her parents allowed only on occasions when they wanted to keep her quiet and happy, or she made up case histories for Shrinks, Incorporated. But today she wanted to stay home.

"Actually," she called to her mother, "I probably don't want to go to the Blue Ridge for a drive."

And as she spoke, she was aware of a plan developing in her mind.

In the back room of her father's office were files of the patients he saw—personal files full of the secrets his patients told him. He kept the file cabinets locked. But Lucy happened to know the key was in the right-hand drawer of his desk in an empty Kleenex box, and the key to his office was kept on a board in the kitchen. If her parents did go on a wildflower trip and agreed to leave Lucy at home alone, she could unlock the office, run upstairs, get the key from her father's desk drawer, unlock the file, and find Cinder's address in a matter of seconds without disturbing any personal secrets whatsoever. Then she and Rosie could take their bikes and ride to Cinder's house.

Dr. Childs was not an unkind man, but he was severe—

sometimes even fierce—and Lucy had admitted to Rosie Treeman that, off and on, she was afraid of him.

"Not that he would spank me or anything," she said to Rosie. "He's absolutely nonviolent," she said to Rosie. "But sometimes I think he would go weeks, even months, without saying a word to me."

"I'd be just as glad if my father didn't speak," Rosie said. "All he says is, 'Did you do your homework? Did you make your bed? Did you do the dishes? Did you comb your hair? Blue jeans are not becoming on girls.' That sort of thing."

"The trouble with my father is that he's English. The English are simply more silent than Americans," Lucy said.

But, she decided, Dr. Childs would never know she had taken the key and gone into his office—unless, as sometimes happened to her, his eyes shot straight through to the center of her brain and he knew what she was thinking. That was the trouble with having a psychiatrist for a father. Rosie's father had no interest whatever in the minds of children—only in their athletic ability, obedience, and domestic chores.

Mrs. Childs wandered into Lucy's room and sat down on the bentwood rocker, looking out the window toward the azalea garden and Dr. Childs's office. She had a look on her face with which Lucy was sadly familiar. The look reminded her that she was excluded from Mrs. Childs's dreams of an afternoon in the country with Dr. Anthony Childs and that secretly she was pleased Lucy had elected to remain at home.

"You're sure you'll be all right at home, Lucy?" she asked.

"Fine," Lucy said.

"Maybe Rosie can come over."

Lucy checked her watch. It was eleven o'clock.

"Now Rosie is at catechism, and then she has to make lunch for her brothers and clean up and do the whites in the laundry and change the beds on the second floor," she said crossly. "By then it will be tomorrow."

"I know I should ask you to do chores, darling." Mrs. Childs lifted Bolivar onto her lap and put him on his back. It was Bolivar's habit since his accident to sleep on his back, upside down with his paws in the air.

"I should have you cook dinner once a week and vacuum, I suppose. My mother used to say it builds character."

"I have as much character as Rosie has already without jobs. Maybe more."

Lucy got out of bed and got dressed in jeans and a red tee shirt that said DOWN WITH FRENCH POODLES on the back.

"What I wish you had done instead of worry about my character was to have another baby."

Mrs. Childs stretched and smiled. This was an old argument with the potential for getting out of hand. Lucy would begin by saying that she wished there had been another child. Mrs. Childs would reply by saying that Lucy had been quite enough to handle. Lucy would then ask why Mrs. Childs had bothered to have any children at all since all she ever wanted to do was to go to the country with Dr. Childs or out to dinner or to a party or a play and Lucy may as well be dead for all she counted. Then Mrs. Childs would say dreamily, and without losing her temper because she never did, that in her next life she was going to have only French poodles. Why don't you get the French poodles *now* instead of waiting around for me to die or grow up, Lucy would say, and Mrs. Childs would smile a strange, faraway smile and say she just might. But the closest the family had come to French poodles was the tee shirt Mrs. Childs had given Lucy on her eleventh birthday. Another baby was simply not a consideration.

"You could have a child now," Lucy said, clipping her bangs with curled fingernail scissors, hoping to drive her mother instantly crazy. "Mrs. Treeman is older than you are by scads and she'll probably have five or six more children, according to Rosie."

"If I did want another child," Mrs. Childs said, depositing Bolivar on his back on Lucy's bed. "I'd adopt." She took the nail scissors gently out of Lucy's hand and dropped them in the pocket of her painting smock.

Lucy's heart leapt up.

Mrs. Childs had never mentioned adopting before; perhaps she could be persuaded.

Before they left for the country, Mrs. Childs made tuna fish sandwiches, and since it was warm, they ate in the garden. Lunch went on and on. Lucy's parents talked about a trip to England and whether to fly Pan Am, which was cheaper, or British Air, which was more loyal, and whether to take Lucy this summer since she had almost died of boredom at her grandmother's the summer before. They talked about vegetables and which ones to plant in the garden this year and whether or not to plant any more melons since they were always squishy or else they didn't grow at all. They talked about a new painting of Mrs. Childs's called *Blue Sky Over the Aegean* which, like most of her paintings, was huge and blue, striped with color, and didn't look a bit like the sea or sky, as far as Lucy could tell. Dr. Childs thought she should raise the price of her paintings to one thousand dollars for a large canvas, and Mrs. Childs blushed as if he had told her she was beautiful. They did not even look at Lucy while they were talking. Instead they held hands right up on the table so Dr. Childs had to cut his tomato salad with a fork.

"I am an abused child," Lucy had once said crossly to her mother after one of these lunches or suppers during which she felt invisible as a ghost.

"Abused?" her mother had asked curiously.

"*Rejected*," Lucy had said. Sometimes they drove her crazy. One thing she knew for a fact was that she would never marry an English psychiatrist or turn into a dreamy-eyed landscape painter with a brain covered in pastels.

Right at this moment, however, all Lucy wanted her parents to do was finish lunch, back the bright red Oldsmobile out of the driveway, and head to the Blue Ridge Mountains without her.

"I'll do the dishes," she said.

"Don't be a martyr," Dr. Childs said.

"I'm not a martyr," she said. "I'm just the ordinary rejected child of a psychiatrist—perfectly normal."

It was two o'clock in the afternoon before the Childses finally left. Mrs. Childs went everywhere prepared. She packed fruit and lemonade, her camera, her sketch book, a first-aid kit, and a change of clothes in case she fell in a creek. Dr. Childs was full of the usual instructions. "Don't go out unless you ask Mrs. Dryer next door. Don't answer the door to strangers"—as if there was more than one stranger a year on Rugby Road. "Don't watch television all day," he said. "And don't use the stove."

"Lucy is almost twelve, darling," Mrs. Childs said. "She'll be fine."

But Dr. Childs was not convinced. He had spent too much of his professional life listening to bad news from children. He did not take chances.

The last thing he said to Lucy before he left the house was not to go into his office.

"Lucy knows that, of course," Mrs. Childs said in exasperation.

"Well, I thought I'd remind her," Dr. Childs said, as if he knew exactly how his daughter planned to spend the day.

Lucy lay down on the living room couch with Bolivar stretched like a blanket across her stomach. She was in a bad mood.

She had planned to go straight to her father's office, unlock the file behind his desk, look up Cinder's address, lock the file, lock the office, get on her bicycle, and then without a word to Mrs. Dryer, take off for Cinder's house. The plan was reasonable and only a little dishonest, she thought to herself. In fact, if Dr. Childs had not mentioned the office as if he could with his X-ray eyes see every terrible thought in Lucy Forever's brain, she never would have worried. Now she imagined he knew exactly what she was going to do and would cancel Shrinks, Incorporated, for good when he returned from his drive in the mountains.

She went into the kitchen, counted out twelve Oreos with double icing, and called Rosie Treeman.

"I hate my brothers," Rosie said sadly. "If all men are like that, I'll never get married."

"Or like my father," Lucy said gloomily, and she told Rosie what had happened.

"Go into his office, anyway," Rosie said coolly. "That's what I'd do," she said. "I'd do it right away without a single Hail Mary or sorry to Jesus or a bit of guilt." And since Rosie was a good, obedient, and religious Catholic girl who believed in God and was absolutely never in trouble at school and did her homework regularly and did not lie to her parents except occasionally to avoid trouble, Lucy Forever took her advice.

She didn't have to search the file cabinet at all. On the top of Dr. Childs's desk was the record for Cinder. Lucy opened the manila folder to the first page. Cinder's address was on the top—846 Cedar Tree Lane. Directly underneath the address Lucy saw *Diagnosis: child abuse* written in pencil in her father's scratchy hand. She closed the folder quickly so she would not be tempted to read on.

Mrs. Dryer was in the garden weeding, as usual, so Lucy went around the side of the house, unlocked her bicycle, and took the long way behind the Abrahams's house to avoid her.

Cedar Tree Lane was a long way to go on a bicycle. Past the University of Virginia, past the town limits of Charlottesville, beyond the place where University Avenue widened and became Route 236 West—a highway well-known to be dangerous for bicycles.

At the corner of Rugby and University, Lucy stopped at the pay phone to call Rosie for moral support. But Mrs. Treeman, who answered out of breath, said that Rosie was at Michael's soccer game and was then going to a church supper at Our Lady of Whatever's and Sunday she would be occupied all day with relatives. Mrs. Treeman liked Lucy very much, but, as she told Rosie, the Childses were not raising their daughter to be a responsible citizen. "Too much freedom," Mrs. Treeman said. Too much freedom sounded like paradise to Rosie, and as far as she could tell Lucy Forever had the luckiest life in the world in spite of being lonely.

Lucy was lonely. She was often lonely on the weekends, especially Sundays, and she wished her mother would seriously consider another child—just a girl to be there while Dr. and Mrs. Childs whispered over lunch together or whisked away in the car to the country. Of course her parents adored her, but she was in the way. They'd be glad for her to go off to college. Probably they were counting the months until she left. Sometimes Lucy envied Rosie's life, with so many relatives and children and visitors that Rosie Treeman seldom had a minute alone except in the bathroom, and even there at least one sister might join her to do her hair or her eyes or her lips before going out on a date.

The afternoon was unseasonably warm, breezeless, too hot for bike-riding up the slopes that led to the foothills of the Blue Ridge. On the steep hills, Lucy dismounted and walked her bicycle. She considered turning back. If she ever made it to Cedar Tree Lane she was going to be too tired for the long ride home. But each time she decided to turn back the small, sad face of the mute child in need of rescue swam in her memory and Lucy was determined to find her.

"Determined" was a word that suited Lucy Childs. Since

first grade, teachers had referred to her determination in their comments, sometimes as a complaint and sometimes as a reference to her lack of cooperation. "Bullheaded" was how the sixth-grade teacher had put it in her last report.

"She means determined," Lucy had said to her father at supper that night.

"Then why didn't she say determined if that's what she meant?" Dr. Childs said, not pleased with Lucy's report card.

"She probably couldn't think of the word," Lucy said absently. "She doesn't have an impressive vocabulary," she added, knowing that Dr. Childs considered an impressive vocabulary one of the few virtues.

"I would describe *you* as bullheaded, darling," Mrs. Childs said sweetly to her husband.

"You would be wrong," Dr. Childs said, pushing his plate away.

"In fact, one of the reasons you are so successful is because you don't give up," she said. "And Lucy is very much like you in that way."

Which is why Lucy Childs finally made it to Cedar Tree Lane in spite of the heat and the long, long ride.

The house was enormous, with a wide balcony and a large columned porch, painted green and in poor repair. There was a small sign on the sidewalk that read "Albemarle County Home for Children." And there, underneath one of the willows surrounding the house, the small mute child sat holding the doll Miss Rosetree had given her on Tuesday.

Lucy stopped her bicycle. No one seemed to be at home. There were no cars in the driveway, no signs of life behind the windows and doors of the large house. Cautiously, she started up the hill.

The child saw Lucy but she did not move. Her eyes were fixed and there was no expression on her face.

"Hello," Lucy said at a distance, not wishing to frighten her. "Remember me?"

Cinder showed no sign of recognition.

"I met you last week," she said quietly. "My office is near Dr. Childs's. You came to visit." She knelt down a few feet away from where the child was sitting. "Remember? Miss Rosetree, my partner, gave you that doll."

Just as she knelt down, however, a loud voice came from the house.

"Don't walk on the grass," the voice said.

The grass did not seem worth considering. Many dark brown weeds with patches of green and yellow sprouted across the long expanse of red clay earth.

"Watch the grass," the voice called again.

Lucy did not reply.

Lucy lay down on her stomach in front of the child, hoping to be hidden from the house by the shadows of willows. She reached out and touched the doll's head.

"You have taken wonderful care of her," she said. "We met this week. Remember? I'm Dr. Forever, and you have made the doll very happy, I can tell."

She didn't hear the front door open or the footsteps on the grass until Mr. Van Dyke, her piano teacher, was standing beside her.

"Lucy Childs," he said, not entirely kindly. "What are you doing so far away from home?"

·4·

Mr. Van Dyke was a long, thin man, pale as wheat stalks, with watery blue eyes and a small chin that disappeared into his neck.

"A man with a weak chin," Dr. Childs had said after Lucy's first piano recital. "Americans have weak chins."

"Your daughter is an American," Mrs. Childs had said crossly.

"American men have weak chins," Dr. Childs said.

Thereafter, Lucy had been fascinated by Mr. Van Dyke's chin. When he sat down on the bench next to her, smelling of last night's supper, she would glance at his chin, which was lavender because the veins were close to the skin and covered like a young duckling in white down.

"You're not listening," Mr. Van Dyke would say. "Please listen carefully. You haven't enough talent to be inattentive."

"You're right," Lucy would say. "I have absolutely no talent." Which was the truth.

"Nice English girls know piano," her father had insisted when she was small.

"I'm not a nice English girl," Lucy had complained to her mother. "And I hate piano."

"You'll just have to take it for one more year."

And one more year and one more year and one more year, Mrs. Childs said every September.

"I hate Mr. Van Dyke," Lucy said. "I'd probably be a very good piano student with another teacher."

"But he's a good piano teacher," Dr. Childs said.

"How do you know that?" Lucy said. "He hasn't taught me anything."

"He has a good reputation," Dr. Childs said.

"I think he's a terrible man," Lucy countered.

But she had never, until this very moment, thought that he was dangerous. Only foolish and slimy, with bad breath and fingers with polished nails long and thin as shish kebab skewers.

Just now, however, as he loomed over Lucy like a giant bird, she was frightened.

"I happened to be talking to Cinder," she said in a small voice.

The mute child, still clutching the doll Rosie Treeman had given her, reached out and touched Lucy's knee. The touch was soft but not accidental, and Lucy looked over at her.

Quietly, with her dark raccoon eyes directly on Lucy, she reached behind her back and lifted a leash just off the grass. To her astonishment, Lucy saw that it attached the child to the broad willow tree.

"Why do you have to tie her up?" she asked Mr. Van Dyke.

"I don't tie her up," Mr. Van Dyke said. "I come three times a week to teach Cinder piano. She has great talent."

"Then why do they tie her up?"

"They don't want to lose her," he said. He untied the leash and walked Cinder into the house. "You come too," he said to Lucy.

The house was enormous, the size of a castle, with ceilings twice the height of ordinary ceilings and a giant fireplace in the living room, large enough for Lucy to stand inside. There was a sweeping double staircase and stained glass windows casting shafts of yellows and blues and reds, pathways to the sun.

"Miss Brill," Mr. Van Dyke called, and the nurse whom Lucy had met before marched down one side of the double staircase.

At the top of the stairs, Lucy saw children, mostly small children, all silent as stone, watching her from between the balusters.

Miss Brill had enormous lips, which made her mouth seem larger than it actually was. Her bones were large and mannish and her eyes too small for such a large head. They were dark eyes, without sympathy for children—Lucy could tell.

"This is Lucy Childs, one of my piano students," Mr. Van Dyke said.

"We have met," the nurse said in a voice that did not promise friendship. "Last Tuesday at her house."

Mr. Van Dyke told the nurse that he was going to skip the piano lesson and take Lucy home.

"I think it's best for her to go home right away," Mr. Van Dyke said, and he gave the nurse a warning look. "I'll come back for Cinder's lesson."

On the trip back to Charlottesville, Lucy tried to make polite conversation, but Mr. Van Dyke was not in a conversational mood. She asked him about the nurse, who he said he did not know well, and about the mute child.

"I suppose she can't talk because her throat was cut."

"She won't talk," Mr. Van Dyke replied. He stopped at the drugstore to buy a large bottle of aspirin and some peanut M&Ms, which he ate without offering her any.

"So," Lucy said. "I suppose that is an orphanage."

"It is the county home for children who either cannot live with their parents or whose parents are dead," Mr. Van Dyke said.

"Are Cinder's parents dead?" Lucy asked.

"I really don't know. I am not in the habit of asking personal questions."

They drove into the Childs's driveway. The sun was going down, and the large tree in front of the house cast ominous shadows that dashed across the lawn as if alive. Lucy wished her parents were there.

"Well," she said brightly. "Thanks for the ride." She hopped out of the car and went around the back to get her bicycle. Mr. Van Dyke did not get out to help her. In fact, he didn't even turn the car engine off until she had gotten her bike and locked it beside the house and was walking up the path to the front door. Then he turned it off and got out.

"I don't need help," Lucy called. "I have the key," she said. "My father's probably working upstairs, and my mother's probably at the market."

Her hand was actually shaking as she tried to put the front door key in the lock. She heard him coming up the walk, and before she had the door unlocked, he grabbed her wrist. Or at least that's what she told Rosie. It *felt* as if he had grabbed her wrist because she was prepared for trouble. In fact, he had only touched her.

"I will have to tell your father that you came out to the home unless you can promise to leave Cinder alone. She is a very troubled child."

"I wasn't bothering her," Lucy said. "I just happened to find her tied to a tree when I was out for a long bike ride."

"That's unlikely," Mr. Van Dyke said crossly. "My guess is that after your parents left today, you looked up her address in your father's files and rode over to Cedar Tree Lane specifically to see her."

"Well," Lucy said, "you happen to be wrong."

"Maybe," Mr. Van Dyke said as he walked back down the path. "But don't let it happen again."

Lucy double-locked the front door, put on the chain, and ran upstairs to the long window in her parents' room, slipping behind the sash curtains to watch Mr. Van Dyke. Somehow she expected him to stay—to wait in the driveway for her parents to return or to try to get in the house. But instead he drove out of the driveway, and Lucy watched the station wagon until it was out of sight.

She didn't like dusk—it made her feel lonely. Sometimes when she was alone in the house, she wished for her parents to divorce so they wouldn't have each other any longer. Then she could have each of them, one at a time, to herself.

"I would love to change places with you," Rosie had often told her. "To have my own room and no brothers. Heavenly bliss," she'd say.

"You'd change your mind after a night alone," Lucy would say sadly.

Lucy picked up Bolivar, held him on her shoulder like a baby, lay down on her mother's side of the bed, and called Rosie.

Mrs. Treeman would not allow Rosie to come to the phone. She was dressing to go to her Aunt Eleanor's, she said.

"Tell her to call me later," Lucy said sadly.

Lucy closed her eyes and imagined a million happy Treemans at a long table full of wonderful homemade food, chattering away like pigeons.

"We don't even have relatives," Lucy had said to her mother when she was particularly cross. "Daddy's stuffy ones are across the ocean and yours are in boxes underground." Which was perfectly true. Most of the relatives Mrs. Childs had ever had were dead.

"Family dinners aren't like that at all," Rosie had told Lucy. "The men get drunk and do all of the talking and think my stupid brothers are funny, and I have to do the dishes. Sometimes Mikey throws up at the table."

"We never have family dinners at all. Just Mother and Daddy staring into each other's eyes and me sitting like a stranger between them."

In the downstairs hall, the grandfather clock struck seven. Seven—and her parents were still in the country. Maybe they had already had supper—a candlelight supper without her at a restaurant with fancy desserts. She went downstairs with Bolivar and checked the refrigerator, which was practically empty—half a can of Progresso minestrone, two hard-boiled eggs, a quart of skim milk, and a strawberry pie from Mrs. Doolittle. Lucy took out the strawberry pie, cut a large slice, and sat down to eat. But all she could eat was the currant glaze on the top of the pie. She was simply too lonely.

She watched the second hand wander slowly around the clock over the stove. By seven-fifteen her parents were still not home. She decided that if they were not home by seven twenty-five, she was going into her father's office to read Cinder's file all the way through. She took the key to the office and stood in front of the clock as it moved slowly to seven twenty-five. Then she turned on the yard light, took the key, opened the back door, and walked down the path to the office. Halfway down the path she heard the telephone, but by the time she had run back, the person had hung up.

She sat down in her father's leather chair and turned on the brass lamp. Open on the oak desk in front of her was a thick red book entitled *Child Abuse* in black letters. She began to read exactly where her father must have been reading. Lydia Simmons was an infant in a suburban home in Chicago, the first child of Mr. and Mrs. Simmons. Before she could even stand, her mother, sometimes her father, tied her legs and arms together, sometimes for a day and a night. This went on for years, and nobody knew until Lydia arrived at kindergarten with bruises all over her body. In October her arm was broken, on Halloween her nose was broken. She looked like a prizefighter. When the teacher asked her what had happened, Lydia invented a complicated story about how she had taken her parents' car and driven it out of the driveway and down the street, crashing into a tree. The second time she came to school with bruises, she insisted she had fallen out of a second-story window trying to get her cat out of a tree. This time the teacher questioned the truth of the story and took her to the principal, who called the welfare agency. Mr. and Mrs. Simmons were caught and arrested and lost Lydia to people who treated her more kindly. Lucy was just beginning to read a second story about child abuse when she heard the door open and her father came into the office waiting room.

"Hello," he called. "Is anyone there?"

Lucy waited.

"Hello," he called again. "Lucy?"

He bounded up the stairs two at a time, through the reception room, and opened the door to his office.

"What are you doing in here?" His face was flushed with anger.

"Reading." She closed the large red book.

"Reading what?" he asked. "You know you are not permitted in here," he said.

"Your book. I need to know about child abuse," Lucy replied and looked at him directly. "You're very late. I suppose you've already eaten dinner."

She followed her father back to the house, picked up Bolivar in the kitchen, and went upstairs to her own room to think about child abuse and how the mute child might have been abused and by whom.

"I'm thinking of moving in with Rosie," she said to her mother when Mrs. Childs came upstairs.

"The Treemans already have too many children, darling." Mrs. Childs sat down on the end of the bed.

"That may be true," Lucy said. "But *you* don't have enough."

°5°

R osie finally called. Lucy was almost asleep when the telephone rang in her parents' room and Dr. Childs knocked on her door.

"Dinner at Aunt Eleanor's was terrible," she said. "I spilled spaghetti on my new yellow dress, and Mikey threw up at the table, of course. What about you?"

So Lucy told Rosie all about Cinder and the leash and Mr. Van Dyke and child abuse.

They agreed to talk on Sunday after lunch and to meet at Shrinks, Incorporated, on Monday afternoon at three.

"It's going to be hard to have regular old made-up patients now that we have a real one," Rosie said wistfully.

"She only comes to see my father once a week," Lucy said, "so we have the whole rest of the week to do absolutely nothing. We'll be glad to have our regular old patients."

"I suppose," Rosie said.

When she hung up the phone, Lucy heard her father call and she went into her parents' bedroom. He was in his pajamas, lying propped up and looking a great deal older than forty-five, with a nest of gray hair curling out of the open pajama top.

"Come on in, Lucy," he said, formal as usual.

She stood beside his bed.

"Perhaps you can tell me why you were reading about child abuse?"

"Curiosity." She looked away from him, out the window at the dark night.

"You don't happen to know of any children at school who have been abused do you?" he asked.

Lucy shook her head. "I don't even have invented abused children in my files at Shrinks, Incorporated," she said. "Until I read your book, I didn't know much about child abuse."

"Did you look at my files?" Dr. Childs asked.

Lucy very seldom lied. Once she had eaten the last of the chocolate chip ice cream in the freezer and said she hadn't. Another time her cousin Billy from Omaha had stolen two packages of peanut M&Ms from Eckart Drugs and was caught. Lucy had said she and Billy were both from Omaha so the clerk wouldn't call her parents, and she'd paid for the M&Ms from her own allowance. And once she had stolen Lily Larker's eraser from her locker. But that was all the lying she could remember, and each time she had felt so terrible that now she considered carefully the temptation to lie whenever it came to her.

"Lucy?"

"No," she said. "I didn't look in your files."

Of course, she thought to herself, that was actually true. She had looked at the files just long enough to copy Cinder's address and only accidentally saw the words *child abuse* under *Diagnosis*. She didn't look *in* the files.

"Why were you in my office?" Dr. Childs was reasonable.

"I suppose I was upset because you and Mother were away."

"And you felt like an abused child?"

Lucy hated it when her father played psychiatrist with her.

"Of course not," she said. "The children in your book were beaten or tied up or worse than that. I am simply left too much to myself."

"Which is good for your imagination," Dr. Childs said. "Most children your age in America watch television day and night and have their imaginations washed right out of their brains."

"My imagination is fine," Lucy said crossly.

"Good night, Lucy. Don't ever go in my office again." He got up and turned off the light. "If you are interested in child abuse, I'll be happy to provide you with books to read about it in your own bedroom."

In bed, staring at the lace designs the streetlights made on the window, she daydreamed about Cinder. In her daydream, Cinder lay on the couch at Shrinks, Incorporated, in a stiff white dress and patent-leather shoes, holding the doll from Miss Rosetree. Her eyes were closed and one small hand covered the scar on her neck.

"Tell me what you are feeling," Dr. Forever said.

"Cold," Cinder said.

"Cold all over? I remember feeling cold—frozen, like I was stuffed in the freezer compartment of the refrigerator. Is that how you feel?"

"Yes," Cinder said, covering her eyes with the doll. "I am outside in the snow all alone in my party dress tied to the tree waiting for my mother. Inside, my nurse and Mr. Van Dyke are having supper at the kitchen table."

"Go on," Dr. Forever said.

"I begin to cry because I am cold and lonely. 'Shut up,' Mr. Van Dyke calls from the house, opening the kitchen window. 'Shut up immediately.' But I can't shut up. Something inside me is broken and I can't stop crying. And then Mr. Van Dyke comes outside with a long silver knife and cuts my throat. Not so much that I die but enough that I bleed a lot."

Lucy rolled over on her stomach and buried her face in the pillow to erase the picture of Mr. Van Dyke cutting Cinder's throat. She could not sleep. She wished above all things that Rosie Treeman had an apartment so she could call her any hour of the night or day. She got up and checked her own clock. It was eleven-thirty. Quietly she opened her bedroom door. The light was on in her parents' room, the door was open. She went down the hall and knocked. Her mother was asleep with her head on her father's shoulder, but she opened her eyes when Lucy walked in.

"Hello, darling," she said. "It's almost tomorrow. Now go to sleep."

Her father was reading an enormous medical book, as he usually did before he went to bed at night.

"I was wondering about something," she said to her

father. "I was wondering if you imagine what is going on in your patient's mind or if they tell you."

"Both," her father said. "Why do you ask?"

"No reason," Lucy said. "Except I can't go to sleep. I keep thinking of the mute child."

"Don't. There's nothing you can do," her father said.

"Get some hot milk, darling." Her mother stretched and yawned and curled like a cat next to her father.

"And think about an ordinary way for a young girl to spend her afternoons instead of pretending to be a psychiatrist. It's tiresome enough being an adult, without trying to grow up too soon," Dr. Childs said. "Why don't you do sports?"

"I don't want to do sports," Lucy said. "Rosie hates sports and I prefer to be with Rosie."

She wanted to ask her father about Mr. Van Dyke but decided against it. Certainly if Mr. Van Dyke were a dangerous man, her father, with his X-ray eyes, ought to have seen that and insisted she change piano teachers.

She went downstairs, took the strawberry pie out of the refrigerator, and cut a large piece for herself and a small piece for Bolivar. Then she put Bolivar on the kitchen table and they ate the pie together.

When Mrs. Childs came downstairs at six, which she often did in order to sit in the living room and watch the way the early morning light fell on the objects in the room, Lucy was asleep on the couch with Bolivar. The growing light cast a yellow shaft over their sweet faces.

In the attic bedroom with her sisters, Rosie Treeman could not sleep. Her older sister, in the bunk above her, had the radio on and was singing in a soprano voice to the Top Ten and tapping her foot so the bed shook. Her younger sister was in trouble for stealing a pack of sugarless gum from Aunt Eleanor's kitchen drawer and had been crying since her spanking hours before. Rosie put a pillow over her head, her fingers in her ears, and thought about Shrinks, Incorporated.

She had two patients in serious trouble. Mary Basil was paralyzed from the waist down ever since her older brother, Sean, had sweetened her cereal with rat poisoning. Mary Basil had had troubles enough before she was poisoned. She had stuttered since birth. "M-m-m-ma, D-d-d-da," she said. She was so afraid of water she could not even take a bath. And every time she went to communion she fainted dead away when the priest put the wafer on her tongue. Sean was also a patient of Miss Rosetree's, sent to her because he had murderous thoughts, but Miss Rosetree decided she was no good at hard-core criminals like Sean and sent him on to Dr. Forever.

"Rosie," her older sister called above the voice of Bruce Springsteen, "could you make Ellie shut up? I can't even hear the music."

"Her bottom hurts," Rosie said, not pleased to have her daydreams interrupted by her miserable older sister.

"No bottom can hurt for two hours unless it's made of pansy petals," she said. "Do something, Rosie, *now*."

"Be quiet," Ellie said. "Everyone be quiet. This is the meanest house in the whole world. If you're such a wonderful psychiatrist, Rosie Treeman, why don't you take care of me?"

Which was all Rosie needed to hear. She got up out of

bed and went over to Ellie's cot by the window overlooking the back of the row house on Second Street. She knelt down next to the bed and ran her fingers through Ellie's tight curly hair. She actually liked her little sister best of everyone in the world except Dr. Forever. So did Lucy.

"Sometimes I wish on chicken bones for a baby sister like Ellie," Lucy would say to Rosie. "But no luck."

Rosie kissed Ellie on the cheek. "It's much easier to be a psychiatrist to made-up people. Then if you want to make them well, you can just decide they are well. Real people aren't so easy," she said.

But she stayed with Ellie until she fell asleep, and when Mrs. Treeman came in to turn off the radio, Rosie too had fallen asleep with her hand on her sister's forehead.

·6·

Mrs. Childs was a gentle, dreamy woman who floated magically through Lucy Forever's life. And Lucy adored her, even though her mother's absent-mindedness drove her crazy. Mrs. Childs's brain was always half absent, painted with the landscape on which she was working in her studio. Frequently she forgot to buy groceries for dinner or lost the car in the parking lot at the A&P or arrived for the PTA meeting on the wrong night.

Lucy loved Sunday mornings in particular, when her mother settled in the living room after breakfast, ready to talk. Sunday was the only day of the week that Mrs. Childs wanted to talk at all, but on these mornings Dr. Childs put on his gardening clothes, took a lawn chair from the porch, and sat in the garden next to his beloved rose bushes to read the paper. He would follow the same routine every Sunday unless it was raining hard or the temperature was below forty degrees. He was a precise man and could be counted on to finish the *New York Times* and the *Charlottesville Daily Progress* in two hours and forty minutes. This was the time Lucy talked with her mother.

On this Sunday morning in early May, Lucy had an

agenda. She settled into the couch next to her mother, covered her feet with her mother's long robe, and asked why it was her father could talk so easily to his patients when he could not talk to her, his daughter, except at a great distance.

"Sometimes I feel as if he is a stranger I met on a bus," Lucy said.

"Your father was brought up very formally in England," Mrs. Childs said. "He doesn't know how to be close."

"Except to you."

"I suppose that's true."

"Then how can he be a psychiatrist?" Lucy asked. "What good is he if he can't be close? I am very close to my patients," Lucy said. "They tell me everything."

"I believe your father's patients tell him quite a lot, too," Mrs. Childs said, "or he wouldn't be known as such a fine psychiatrist."

"Maybe," she said.

Lucy did remember a visit with her father to Swensen's for a double-dip butter pecan cone when a pretty woman standing in line behind them grabbed Dr. Childs's hand.

"I am so glad to see you," she said. "You saved my life."

"How did you save her life?" Lucy asked once they were in the car.

"I didn't save her life," he said. "Psychiatrists don't save lives. Other doctors do, but not psychiatrists. She saved her own life and she ought to know better than to blame me for it."

Lucy ate her ice cream in silence and didn't ask any more questions. Sometimes her father was simply too peculiar.

"I suppose he is a fine psychiatrist." Lucy pulled her knees up under her chin. "How do you think he can find out anything about the mute child if she doesn't talk?"

"What he knows about her is that something terrible happened to make her stop talking, and he hopes to discover that."

"Have you seen him work with patients?"

"Of course not, darling. But I have been to a psychiatrist once before you were born because I was very sad not to have a child."

"Tell me what happens when you go to see one." Lucy had never been to a psychiatrist. She had made up what she did as a doctor for Shrinks, Incorporated, by listening to other psychiatrists, friends of her father, talk at the dinner table. She had visited her father's office and played with the games he had for children and tried out the couch where the older children lay down to talk with Dr. Childs. She had even read through some of the articles he had written on patients—she remembered one on bed-wetters—but she had only imagined what a psychiatrist was supposed to do. What she imagined a psychiatrist was supposed to be was a wonderful mother like her own who did not paint landscapes but spent all of her days listening to every word her child said. That was the kind of psychiatrist she was at Shrinks, Incorporated, except with impossible patients like Mrs. Parks.

Mrs. Childs sat down on a yellow flowered wing chair across from Lucy. "Would you like to practice? I'll show you how it works. I'm Daddy and you are Lucy Childs in deep trouble."

"What deep trouble?" Lucy asked.

"You tell me," Mrs. Childs said. She assumed a serious expression, unsmiling, earnest, and looked directly at Lucy Forever.

"My parents love each other better than they love me," Lucy said. "They would rather go off together on a trip to the mountains alone than to have me along. Sometimes I want to run away from home."

"Darling, that's not true," Mrs. Childs said, stricken. "We adore you."

Lucy smiled and raised her eyebrows at her mother. "I thought you were supposed to be a psychiatrist," she said. "*Everything* I say is true if I'm your patient. You have to be on my side. That's what Annie Myers told me, and she's gone to a psychiatrist since she was four years old. She's a serious case."

"I am on your side, absolutely," Mrs. Childs said. "You are my darling daughter."

"I'm not your darling anything. I'm your patient."

Mrs. Childs got up and left the living room. "We'll start again," she said. "I am Dr. Childs and you are Lucy in deep trouble." She came back into the living room imitating Dr. Childs's long, ambling gait.

She sat down in the chair again. "How are you feeling today, Lucy?" she asked in an impersonal voice.

Lucy didn't answer.

"Sad?"

Lucy folded her legs under her and rested her chin in her hands.

"You have a sad look in your eyes, as if you are remembering an unhappy time."

Lucy pulled a clump of long hair and stuck the end of it in her mouth. She crossed her eyes.

"Tell me, did you have a fight with your mother this morning?"

Lucy stared at a painting of tulips above her mother's head.

"Your father? I remember when I was a child being very angry at my mother for painting my bedroom pale yellow and getting rid of my puppy, who ate my grandmother's crocheted pillow. I didn't speak to her for two weeks. Not even good morning."

"Daddy wouldn't tell me a story about himself," Lucy said. "Psychiatrists don't tell *anything* about their own lives."

"But you weren't talking," Mrs. Childs said.

"I was pretending to be Cinder."

Mrs. Childs put Bolivar off the coffee table, where he was drinking the water from a vase of roses. Then she went to the kitchen and took a roast out of the freezer for supper. Lucy followed her.

"I simply don't know how Daddy will find out anything about that poor mute child. It must be a very difficult job to be a psychiatrist."

"He has X-ray eyes," Lucy said.

"I doubt it."

Lucy hopped up on the kitchen table. "I bet I could make that child talk." She opened the funnies.

"Don't try, darling," Mrs. Childs said, knowing very well what Lucy had in mind. "Please don't try."

"Oh I won't, of course," Lucy said. But already she had plans for Cinder the following Tuesday.

·7·

Tuesday morning was dark and rainy, with storm clouds lying like army blankets over the houses on Rugby Road, and Lucy did not want to go to school. She hadn't finished her homework for language arts, so she would have to miss recess again. She had a test in mathematics, and they were doing softball, her worst sport, in gym. Shortly after the alarm went off, she heard the telephone ring in her parents' room and simply expected for no reason at all that the call was going to be trouble. She pushed deep into her bed under the covers so her body made a small lump in the center of her bed. Then she heard her father come into her room.

"Lucy?"

She didn't reply.

"It's after seven," he said in a severe voice, and she felt him push Bolivar off her bed.

"Lucy?"

She stirred and rolled on her side. "I believe I'm quite sick," she said in a feeble voice.

He was not impressed.

"That was Mr. Van Dyke on the telephone," Dr. Childs said.

"I am really very sick," Lucy said weakly. "I probably ought to be in the hospital."

"Mr. Van Dyke called to tell me you have cancelled piano for the next month in order to see a psychiatrist."

"Mr. Van Dyke is a wimp." She sat up against the headboard. "I suppose it doesn't matter that I'm sick."

"I don't believe you are sick."

"Well, Mr. Van Dyke is a liar. I don't know what's the matter with him. He's simply not a very trustworthy man."

"Apparently not, since you told him specifically not to mention the psychiatrist to me."

Lucy got out of bed and went to her closet. "I'm probably going to throw up," she said. At least Mr. Van Dyke hadn't told Dr. Childs about her visit to Cinder's.

"Get dressed for school," Dr. Childs said. "If you do get sick, then the nurse can contact us."

She picked out a white tee shirt with a panda bear on the back and blue shorts and her tennis shoes and went into the bathroom. She braided her hair in a French braid with a yellow ribbon. She examined her nose in the mirror over the sink as she often did to see if it was growing into the awful nose her English grandmother spread with peach-colored powder every morning. By the time she was dressed, she had decided what to tell her father, which was the truth. In part.

He was sitting on the end of her bed reading the first half of her language arts paper on *To Kill a Mockingbird*, which happened to be the only half she had written.

"The fact is I told Mr. Van Dyke the truth," she said, hoping very much to look as sick as she was feeling. "I didn't want you to know I was going to see a psychiatrist because I was afraid you'd feel like a failure."

"I see," Dr. Childs said. "That was thoughtful of you, Lucy. However, I have no problems with failure." He got up to leave the bedroom. "I did tell Mr. Van Dyke you'd be at piano today as usual."

At breakfast, Dr. Childs read the paper.

"It's raining," Lucy said, pushing her bowl of cereal away. "I hate to walk to school in the rain."

"In England it rains almost every day," her father said, folding the paper to the editorial page.

"I hate England."

"It's your heritage," Dr. Childs said into the paper.

When the telephone rang it was Rosie, arranging to meet her at the drug store on Main and walk to school.

"I just *know* I'm getting the stomach flu," she said.

Dr. Childs did not look up.

"I suppose in England children go to school with the stomach flu," she said to her father. But he was deeply involved in a story on the financial page and didn't reply.

"Are you interested in finding out why I need to see a psychiatrist?" she asked her father combatively.

"Of course I'm interested but it's not my business," he said. "The relationship between a psychiatrist and his patient is private."

"Brother," Lucy said, taking a piece of toast. "I'm your daughter, not a patient."

"Of course, darling," Dr. Childs said, and he smiled his secret smile, which always meant to Lucy that he understood everything in the world.

She made a point of kissing Bolivar goodbye and complained loudly that her raincoat wasn't waterproof, nor was her book bag, and she wished her mother would wake up in time for breakfast sometimes instead of sleeping all day.

"When I'm a real psychiatrist, at least I'll be understanding of my own children," she said to Rosie as they marched through the rain to school.

"I'm not having children," Rosie said.

"I'll probably have eight."

"Well, you'll be sorry," Rosie said. "And that's a promise."

"I'll meet you at three-thirty exactly," Lucy said as they parted in the main corridor of Haddenfield Elementary.

As it turned out, Miss Grace made Lucy stay after school in language arts to finish her paper on justice in *To Kill a Mockingbird*. She even offered to let her stay until five to redo the entire paper so she wouldn't receive a "D."

"No thanks," Lucy said when she completed the first draft. "A 'D' is fine. I don't mind at all."

And she raced out of the classroom, down the steps, across Elm Street, up University to Main, where she had to walk because the sidewalk was full of students from the University of Virginia carrying umbrellas. At Rugby, she turned and ran home. No doubt Miss Grace had already called her mother. "Mrs. Childs," Miss Grace would say. "Your daughter Lucy is going to fail sixth grade." She arrived at her house just as the nurse who takes care of Cinder was leaving in her yellow station wagon.

Mrs. Childs was on the front steps as Lucy raced by.

"Lucy," she called.

"I'm in a terrible hurry," Lucy said. "I'm very late."

Mrs. Childs followed her upstairs to her bedroom, where she took off her panda tee shirt and navy shorts, took the rubber band out of her French braid, slipped on stockings with large runs, a pair of dyed pink satin high heels, and a red silk dress, and did her hair quickly in a floppy bun.

"Miss Grace just called."

Lucy put on blush and lipstick and lavender eyeliner.

"What a surprise," Lucy said.

Mrs. Childs sat in the rocking chair next to Lucy's bed.

"She isn't pleased with your work in language arts or your attitude, darling."

"She's a terrible teacher, Mother. I'd learn more from a golden retriever." She put a belt around her waist to keep the skirt off the floor and started down the steps.

"Darling."

"I'm not darling," she said. "I'm Dr. Forever on my way to the office and I'm very late."

Miss Rosetree sat primly at her desk. She was on the telephone.

"Yes," she said.

"Yes, I understand."

"Dreadful," she said.

"That's the worst news I've ever heard."

She rolled her eyes at Dr. Forever.

"No, I've never treated anyone under a year old. I'm very sorry. Perhaps you should call Dr. Forever. Yes, she's here now."

Dr. Forever picked up the telephone.

"Dr. Forever speaking," she said.

"Yes," she said.

"Yes, I understand."

"Dreadful," she said.

"That's the worst news I've ever heard."

"Of course I'm willing to treat small children under a year old. I will even treat cats and dogs. Can you bring him right over?"

She hung up the telephone.

"So," she said to Miss Rosetree. "That's the mother whose baby thinks he is an opossum?"

"Exactly," Miss Rosetree said. "I really don't like the animal cases any longer. I'm getting too old. I'll only take care of people who know very well that they're people."

Miss Rosetree went into the back room and took off her paisley dress, put on a blue silk and lace top and half glasses and yellow wig, and ran up the stairs, through the house, out the front door, around to the side, and knocked at the door of Shrinks, Incorporated.

"Come in," Dr. Forever said.

"I'm in, I'm in," Miss Rosetree said, falling through the door in a small heap on the floor. "I am Angelica Brainchild and this is my son, Harry, who thinks he's an opossum. Say hello to Dr. Forever, Harry. Say it in English."

"Hello, Harry," Dr. Forever said. "No wonder he thinks he's an opossum, Mrs. Brainchild. He looks exactly like one."

Lucy pretended to lift Harry from the floor.

"So, Harry, how was it being an opossum when everybody was expecting a little boy?" She made a face. "Does Harry always smell like this, Mrs. Brainchild?"

"Always." Mrs. Brainchild sat on a chair across from Dr. Forever's desk and wept. "Sometimes worse," she confessed.

"That's unfortunate." She handed the imaginary baby opossum back to Mrs. Brainchild and took a stenographic pad out of her desk. "Tell me *everything*, Mrs. Brainchild."

"Harry is my first child," Mrs. Brainchild said breathlessly. "He was born when I was sixty-one years old."

"That's quite old."

"Yes," Mrs. Brainchild agreed. "But I didn't get married until I was sixty."

"I see."

"No one would marry me because I was so ugly."

"I certainly understand," Dr. Forever said.

"You think I'm ugly?" Mrs. Brainchild asked. "I knew you would. Everyone does. In fact, my husband said I reminded him of a squirrel."

"Let's get back to Harry."

"Well, Harry was wonderful in every imaginable way, a perfectly normal baby boy who looked a little peculiar. When he was three months old, however, I noticed that he began to make opossum sounds."

"What is an opossum sound?"

Mrs. Brainchild squeaked sadly.

"I see."

"And then he began to bite."

"Is that why you have teeth marks all over your body?"

"I'm afraid so," Mrs. Brainchild said. "And then he

began to look exactly like an opossum, as you can very well see for yourself."

"This is very sad."

"What am I to do?" Mrs. Brainchild asked.

"I know exactly what you should do, Mrs. Brainchild. You should purchase an opossum from a pet shop and bring him home so Harry will begin to understand that the opossum is an opossum and that he is a little boy. Simple as that."

"I don't want an opossum," Mrs. Brainchild cried. "Already I have one opossum too many."

"Then I am afraid I can be of no help to you." She got up, closed her notebook, and picked up the telephone. "Dr. Forever speaking. No, I'm terribly sorry. My partner, Miss Rosetree, is in intensive care at the University of Virginia Hospital with a case of fleas."

"Lucy?" Miss Rosetree said. She never called Lucy anything but Dr. Forever when they were working at Shrinks, Incorporated. "What time is it? I'm tired of playing."

Lucy checked her Mickey Mouse watch. It was ten to five, almost exactly the time that Dr. Childs would be finishing with the mute child. Exactly what they had been waiting for.

"Time," Lucy said.

They went to the basement window that overlooked the backyard and waited. They waited and waited. At five o'clock Rosie looked at Lucy.

"What do you think could have happened?"

Lucy shook her head.

"Do you think we could have missed her?"

"I don't think so," Lucy said

"Maybe she got worse while she was in his office," Rosie said. "Maybe she turned into some kind of animal."

"Maybe."

"Maybe she went into a coma."

Lucy looked at her friend strangely. "You have entirely too much imagination. Why don't you check outside to see if the nurse has come back to pick her up?"

It was five after five. Rosie walked out the door of Shrinks, Incorporated, into the dark drizzle of late afternoon, down the pebble driveway to Rugby Road. She didn't see the yellow station wagon. Probably, she thought to herself, they had missed the mute child entirely. She had left her appointment with Dr. Childs early. Maybe she had even *talked* to Dr. Childs and he let her go since she told him everything that had happened to her. Now they'd have to wait for a whole week to see her again. These were the thoughts in Rosie Treeman's mind as she passed the large rhododendron in full pink bloom beside the entrance of Shrinks, Incorporated, and noticed a splash of bright yellow behind the bush. She looked more carefully as she passed. When the splash of yellow moved, Rosie opened the door to Shrinks, Incorporated, closed it quietly behind her, and went straight over to Dr. Forever, who was on the telephone with St. Elizabeth's Hospital for Entirely Crazy People.

"Lucy?"

"Dr. Forever," Lucy said crossly, putting her hand over the receiver. "Can't you see I'm on an emergency call?"

"She's behind the rhododendron bush," Rosie said.

Lucy dropped the telephone and stood up.

"And the nurse is nowhere in sight."

"What'll we do?" Lucy asked.

"Tell her to come in, of course," Rosie said.

"No, we've got to be more careful than that," Lucy said. "We'll just go outside and have a conversation and pretend to be checking the weather or a dead patient under the rhododendron bushes or something like that. I'll say 'Do you think we can have a picnic tonight with this rain, Miss Rosetree?' and you'll say 'I doubt it.' And if she doesn't come out then I'll say 'Do you think Mrs. Apple died under the rhododendron or the apple tree and should we call an ambulance or look for her ourselves?' "

"Brother. Those are dumb conversations." Rosie opened the door.

And there she was. She stood directly in front of the door in a yellow slicker that covered half her face. She was holding her belly, which seemed to stick out as if she were pregnant.

"Oh hello," Lucy said. "I'm very glad to see you again."

"We were just going to check the weather to see if it was too rainy to have a picnic tonight, weren't we, Dr. Forever?"

"Too rainy," Lucy said, shaking her head.

"Maybe tomorrow," Rosie said. "And maybe you can come with us on a picnic."

The child looked up with a quizzical expression.

"We go to the park. It's quite a lot of fun. There're slides and seesaws and swings," Rosie said. "Have you been to the park?"

The child stepped into the open basement room, still holding her broad stomach.

"There's a lovely park just down the hill with a pond and ducks."

Cinder seemed to be interested. She looked right at Miss Rosetree and Dr. Forever and seemed to understand, although she certainly didn't reply.

Rosie saw the nurse first. She walked up the driveway and came straight to the office of Shrinks, Incorporated, as if she knew exactly where the mute child was.

"I supposed I would find you here," she said to the child, her voice like a volcano.

Because she was directly in front of the child Lucy noticed an expression of horror fly across Cinder's face. The little girl lifted one hand to the nurse and took the other one off her belly. As she did, the baby doll that Rosie had given her the week before fell from beneath her raincoat.

Neither Lucy nor Rosie picked it up, but Lucy did lean down and shake the small plump hand gently. As she did, the child made a sound in her throat very much like the sound of the opossum.

"She's brought back the doll you gave her," the nurse said, walking out the door with Cinder. "She doesn't need it. She has hundreds of dolls already, don't you, Cinder?"

There was a moment's pause.

"She says yes. Hundreds."

Rosie and Lucy stood side by side and watched the nurse in her black rain poncho and Cinder in her bright yellow slicker walk down the driveway and get into the station wagon parked on Rugby Road. Then Rosie walked back to the place where Cinder had been and picked up the doll.

It was the same doll Rosie had given the child, but she

had on a different dress, a new one with roses and a lace collar. Just as Rosie was about to put the doll in the trunk with other dolls and costumes, she noticed something.

"Lucy?" Rosie said, handing the doll to Dr. Forever. "Look."

Lucy took the doll.

"She slashed her throat," Rosie said. There was a slash across the doll's rubber neck that went straight through the rubber to the hollow space beneath.

"Creepy," Lucy said. She put the doll on top of the trunk.

Rosie sat in the office chair beside her desk, put her chin in her hand, and thought while Lucy went upstairs to get Oreos and to check the mail in case her report card had come. When she came back downstairs with fourteen Oreos and two peanut butter cookies and chocolate milk, Rosie was inspecting the doll's neck.

"Dr. Forever," she said. "I believe that child is sending us a message." And they sat on Lucy's desk eating Oreos in silence.

·8·

Mr. Van Dyke lived in a brick row house across from the University of Virginia, where he taught the theory of musical composition to university students. From time to time in the last four years since Lucy had begun the hopeless task of studying piano with him, he had tried to teach her music theory or elements of composition, and on these occasions, especially when she was younger, Lucy cried. Then mild-mannered, sweet-tempered Mr. Van Dyke turned into a trapped rat.

"You have no ear," he'd hiss. "God must have given you plastic ears." Or "How did you ever get out of first grade without being able to read?"

"I do read," Lucy would say.

"*Music*," Mr. Van Dyke would scream so loudly the pictures in the living room shook. "You don't read *music*."

Once, when he was explaining to her the patterns of chords, droning on and on, she tipped over in her chair and hit her head. That time he lost control completely. He danced around the room like a child, stamping his feet, his face bright pink with fury.

"Go home, go home," he said.

"I am going home," Lucy said very calmly, "but I have a concussion."

These outbursts, however, were infrequent. Once or twice she had mentioned them to her mother, who said that artists like Mr. Van Dyke are temperamental and should be ignored.

"Mr. Van Dyke is not an artist," Lucy had said. "He's a wimp."

And mostly he *was* a wimp. Mostly he sat on the piano bench next to her, his head rocking a little foolishly with the music, his long-fingered, blue-veined hands on the piano keys while he waited for the hour with Lucy Childs to be over.

Now, as Lucy walked down Rugby Road, she thought about Mr. Van Dyke's bad moods. Certainly he had every reason to be in a bad mood with her now, and she wondered how the afternoon with him would go.

Even in fair weather, Mr. Van Dyke's house was dark, but on a stormy afternoon it was like a funeral parlor. The front door led straight to the living room, which was empty except for a brown corduroy couch and a grand piano. The walls were covered with pictures, photographs of his family. Once, while Mr. Van Dyke was in the bathroom, she had looked at the pictures. There was not a single one of Mr. Van Dyke—only people who had lived long ago and wore high collars and long dresses—but they all looked exactly like him. It was creepy.

She sat down on the piano bench, put up her music, and played—very badly—the Beethoven piece she had been given to memorize the week before.

"Did you practice, Lucy?" he asked, knowing very well the answer.

Lucy hesitated. She never practiced. Occasionally, if her mother was feeling particularly motherly, she would make Lucy practice once on a Monday afternoon, but usually, to Dr. Childs's fury, she forgot.

"Not a bit," Lucy said matter-of-factly.

"So it sounds," Mr. Van Dyke said. "I have spoken to your father about the psychiatrist," he said out of the blue. She was not expecting to be confronted.

"So he said."

"Your father has no information on a psychiatrist."

Lucy hesitated.

"Did you make that up?"

"No," Lucy said.

"No?" He sat down on the piano bench and hung his fingers over the piano keys. "You're a peculiar girl," he said.

"Are you ready for me to do that piece again?" she asked.

"Of course," he said.

She began to play.

"Too fast," he said. "Start again."

She started again. She played a page and a half of the score, all the time thinking of Mr. Van Dyke and the mute child and what he must know about her life. Then she stopped in the middle, put her hands in her lap and asked Mr. Van Dyke straight out and without so much as a glance in his direction why Cinder had a scar on her throat.

He didn't reply right away. He got up and walked over to the hall table where he kept the house keys and some change, slips of paper with telephone numbers, multiple vitamins, and a roll of Tums for the tummy. He opened the roll of Tums and took two, biting them with his little squirrel teeth. Then he stood next to the piano and looked at Lucy Childs without friendship.

"Leave that child alone," he said.

Lucy studied the score on the piano in front of her.

"Did you hear me, Lucy?"

She turned the page and with her right hand played the melody.

"We are all working hard to help Cinder overcome her fears so she can talk again," Mr. Van Dyke said, "and you could ruin everything."

Lucy stood up, closed the score, picked up her backpack, and stood beside the piano bench.

"*I quit*," she said.

He followed her to the front door.

"You don't need to quit, Lucy. I refuse to teach you any longer." He opened the door for her.

"I'm calling your mother," he said.

Lucy walked down the front steps. "You can call her every hour if you'd like," she said.

At home that evening, her parents said nothing whatsoever to Lucy until bedtime. Her father talked at dinner about a convention of psychiatrists in Montreal and said he was going to take Lucy and Mrs. Childs along with him. Her mother said Aunt Frieda had shingles, her mother's dog had been put to sleep on his twenty-first birthday, and she had ordered 150 perennials for nineteen dollars from a garden catalogue. For supper they had cold salmon and cu-

cumbers, and Dr. Childs said the salmon reminded him of England and he wanted to go in August to visit his family. No wonder she hated to be an only child, Lucy thought as she listened to her parents' dull conversation sail back and forth over her head.

"I quit piano for good today," she said during dessert.

"No doubt it was high time," Dr. Childs said.

She didn't ask if Mr. Van Dyke had called, and they didn't tell her.

She called Rosie after she had done her math and French homework, but Rosie was at the emergency room with her brother John, who had been in a fight with her brother Thomas and had to get his lip stitched up. She was just climbing into bed to read a Sweet Dreams romance when her parents walked in together. She knew by the expressions on their faces that she was in trouble.

Her father sat on the rose-print wing chair across from her bed, and her mother sat on the bentwood desk chair. Her father began to talk.

"Mr. Van Dyke called," he began, not surprisingly.

"He's a creep."

"No doubt," Dr. Childs said, "but he called to say he couldn't teach you piano any longer because you were prying into his personal life."

"He's wrong," Lucy said, wrapping her arms around her legs. "He's wrong more times than anyone I know."

"He says you stopped by the home where the mute child lives on the Saturday when we were in the country."

"By chance I happened to see her when I was out on a bike ride."

"You couldn't have been at Cedar Tree Lane on a bike ride by chance, Lucy. It's too far away."

Lucy hesitated.

"The mute child was tied to a tree," Lucy said. "She was tied to a tree with a dog leash."

"I see," Dr. Childs said, and Lucy could tell that he was genuinely interested in this information.

"I think Mr. Van Dyke is dangerous," Lucy said, taking advantage of her father's curiosity. "I think he may have something to do with the fact that Cinder is mute."

Dr. Childs got the familiar faraway look in his eyes that Lucy always imagined had to do with the fact that he was examining the inside of someone's brain, and then he got up and ran his fingers through his thinning hair and shook his head.

"I will tell you some things I know about Cinder," he said softly. "Three years ago Cinder was up for adoption from an agency in Washington, D.C., because her parents had been killed in an automobile accident. No one adopted her so she was sent to Charlottesville by a social worker to live in the Albemarle County Home for Children, which is run by the nurse with whom you have seen Cinder come to my office. Until this past summer, according to everyone, she was a perfectly normal little girl. Trouble developed this summer when a new child from a difficult background joined the home and was cruel to Cinder. Just before he was to be sent back to his family, Cinder was discovered by Miss Brill with her throat cut. And since that time, she hasn't spoken. The boy denied that he cut Cinder, but he was sent to reform school. In September Mr.

Van Dyke was hired by a group I know to teach her piano in the hope that it would build her confidence." He looked at himself in the mirror over Lucy's dresser. "She came to see me because I have a reputation as a specialist with children who have been through trauma."

"Have you always been successful with children who have been through trauma?" Lucy asked.

"More or less, until now."

Mrs. Childs sat in the chair doing needlepoint.

"You should not have angered Mr. Van Dyke, darling. It simply wasn't kind," she said.

"I suppose I shouldn't." She turned to her father. "I have wondered sometimes if I could get Cinder to talk."

Her father didn't respond exactly.

In a way, Lucy decided as she lay in bed trying to sleep, her father had said, "Yes, go ahead. Try it." At least he hadn't said no.

She began to imagine possibilities.

The room next to her bedroom was a study. Just before Lucy went to sleep, in her mind she redecorated the study in yellow with a canopy bed and a flowered rug, just right for a five-year-old girl who had been adopted by a famous psychiatrist and his painter wife and his psychiatrist daughter.

· 9 ·

At eight on Wednesday morning, before Lucy left for school, she typed a letter on plain paper using her mother's Smith-Corona electric typewriter.

"Dear Miss Brill," it began. "For the next week I will be seeing Cinder for a double session. You can drop her off at my office at four and pick her up at six. Thank you. Best wishes, Anthony Childs, M.D."

Rosie thought the letter was terrific. "Perfect," she said to Lucy Forever. "Now what?"

"Now," Lucy said, walking happily along University Avenue next to her best friend and colleague, "we have Cinder to ourselves for one whole hour every day—if the nurse believes that letter and my father doesn't find it first."

And she told Rosie her game plan.

"You leave school at dismissal, take the letter, run to my house, pin it on my father's door right under the door knocker, and meet me at Shrinks, Incorporated, at around three-thirty."

"What if your father finds it first?"

"That's the chance we have to take," Lucy said.

"And what if the nurse thinks the note is forged?"

"We have to take a lot of chances, as you can see."

"Or comes back before six and finds us with Cinder?" Rosie shook her head. "What if Cinder tells on us? We could be in a lot of trouble, Lucy."

"Cinder doesn't talk. She's not going to suddenly decide to talk just so she can tell on us."

Lucy could tell that Rosie didn't like her game plan very much.

"I'd sort of prefer to go back to being an imaginary psychiatrist," Rosie said. "I really hate trouble."

"We are doing exactly what a real psychiatrist would do if he was still a child. If you're not a detective, how can you find out people's secrets?"

But Rosie was not convinced.

She did, however, do what she was told. At three o'clock dismissal, while Lucy was redoing her paper on *To Kill a Mockingbird*, Rosie ran to the Childs's house, pinned the note to the door of Dr. Childs's office, slipped through the side entrance to the basement of Shrinks, Incorporated, dressed in her paisley polyester office dress, and sat down at her desk to wait for Dr. Forever.

Probably, she thought to herself, *she* was going to be the one who was caught. Dr. Childs would leave his office on some emergency, find the note, and storm into Shrinks, Incorporated, in his stormy way. There Rosie would be, all alone, caught without Lucy. Or else the nurse would arrive in a temper, pick Rosie up under her arms, put her in the back of the yellow station wagon, and drive to some deserted country road where she'd leave her. Or else the mute child would talk. All of a sudden and out of the blue, she would tell everything including her visits to Shrinks, Incorporated. By the time Lucy actually arrived, flying down the basement steps with her panty hose around her knees, her dress unbuttoned, and her hair still in braids, Rosie had made herself sick with worry.

"I quit," she said in a tiny voice.

Lucy pulled her stockings up, put on her glassless glasses, and sat down at her desk.

"You can't quit now, Miss Rosetree. It's altogether too late."

"I think I'm going to be sick."

Lucy dialed a telephone number and waited. "Hello. This is Dr. Forever," she said self-assuredly. "My partner, Miss Rosetree, has one of those made-up sicknesses she gets from time to time, severe hypochondria, and I think you should send an ambulance and take her to St. Elizabeth's for the week."

"Stop it, Lucy," Rosie said. "I won't play."

Dr. Forever looked at her sadly. "You actually look very sick to me today, Miss Rosetree. A serious case, I'm afraid. I wish I were a better psychiatrist, but you look very much as if you have completely lost your mind."

"I would prefer to play rock stars again. I'd even prefer to take up sports," Rosie said with tears in her voice.

"Let me check your pupils," Lucy said without paying a bit of attention. She went over and lifted the lid of Rosie's left eye. "It's a lucky thing I've sent for an ambulance. You have the most serious case of insanity I've seen in years."

"I know we're going to get into trouble," Rosie said, taking off her paisley dress, her high-heeled shoes.

But Dr. Forever had gone to the window, where she saw

the mute child, in a white dress with a yellow sash, holding the nurse's hand. Dr. Forever watched as the nurse took the note off the door and stuffed it in the pocket of her uniform. She opened the door and waited for Cinder to go inside and then she left. As she passed the window she seemed to be smiling as if she had just received good news.

"We're not going to get into trouble," Dr. Forever said. "We've made it."

"How do you know?" Rosie asked. She wanted to go home and do the dishes or polish the furniture or feed the cats, something in a hurry to make up for her sins.

"I just know," Lucy said.

"What if the nurse comes back early?" Rosie asked.

"She won't," Lucy said.

"How do you know all of these things? You aren't even Catholic."

"I know them, Rosie. Believe me."

And Lucy was right.

Miss Rosetree got dressed again in her paisley dress and high heels, pinned the bun on the back of her head, and they waited.

The hour went on and on. They could not pretend to be psychiatrists or call their imaginary patients on the phone or see them or find new ones. They were too excited. They simply waited, standing by the window until finally, finally Cinder opened the door of Dr. Childs's office and stepped outside. She closed the door carefully behind her, walked down the three steps, and, in a determined fashion, walked along the pebble driveway to the door of Shrinks, Incorporated, and stopped. She didn't knock. She simply waited.

"What are we going to do?" Rosie asked.

"Open the door, of course," Lucy said.

"She didn't even look around for her nurse," Rosie said. "It's as if she knew."

"Maybe she does," Lucy said. "Maybe she senses exactly what's going on and wants to tell us something."

When Rosie opened the front door, Cinder stood with one hand loosely over her eyes and the other extended.

"Can I help you?" Lucy asked.

The child dropped her hand from her eyes and made a cradle of her arms, rocking them.

"Would you like the doll back?"

The child nodded.

Rosie got the doll. "We were just making a picnic," she said.

The child took the doll and tucked her under her arm.

"I'll make the picnic." Lucy ran up the stairs. "We'll go to the park with swings." In the kitchen, she got a basket, the remaining Oreo cookies, four soft pears, and her mother's last bottle of Diet Coke. That was all there was in the refrigerator. Lucy packed the small picnic and raced back down the stairs.

To her great surprise, the mute child was lying on the couch as if she were a grown-up patient in a real psychiatrist's office. Her arms rested beside her body, and the doll with the slit neck lay across her face covering her eyes.

Miss Rosetree gave Dr. Forever a warning look.

Rosie had a friend in catechism who was a hypnotist. A professional hypnotist, the friend said. She was actually the daughter of a professional hypnotist who made her living in Charlottesville by treating people who wanted to stop smoking or lose weight or get over their fear of flying or elevators or closed-in places. And for fifty cents, Rosie's friend, who had learned her mother's tricks, hypnotized her classmates. She hypnotized Rosie every Saturday during catechism, and so far, although it had been going on for three months, Sister Mary Michael had no suspicions. In the middle of catechism, Rosie would ask to be excused to go to the ladies' room and, minutes later, Sally Sweet would ask to be excused to talk to Father James about a problem. They'd meet in the basement bathroom, which was used only by the janitor, who didn't work on Saturday mornings. There Sally Sweet would hypnotize Rosie in ten minutes and then they'd go back to catechism. Sally Sweet was very good at it. She had a low, swinging voice and a way about her that made Rosie calm. Then she had a silver cross on a long chain, which she would swing back and forth in front of Rosie's eyes. "You're going to sleep," she'd say in her swinging voice. "Shut your eyes. You're going to sleep." Over and over, she'd repeat the lines until her voice dropped into a hole too deep to see the bottom and Rosie's mind floated out of the world. So far, Rosie had conquered all of her serious problems through hypnosis except the fact that she didn't like most of her brothers, which Sally said was beyond changing. Now Rosie could eat squishy vegetables without gagging. She wasn't afraid of German shepherds. She didn't have a stomachache before communion, and she hadn't choked on a white wafer for weeks.

"Why don't you do me?" Lucy asked Rosie from time to time.

"I can't," Rosie said. "You have to have some kind of

magic powers that I don't have. I'm really a very ordinary psychiatrist."

"Ask Sally Sweet to teach you."

"She won't. I know she won't," Rosie said. But she had tried out hypnosis on her younger brothers and it had worked, particularly with Sammy Boy, who wanted to stop wetting his bed—with good reason, since he was already nine years old.

When Lucy walked into the office, Rosie had already hypnotized the mute child and was seated in a chair beside her talking in the same low swinging voice she had learned from Sally Sweet.

"You are going to talk," she sang quietly.

Lucy sat down in the corner on the picnic basket to listen.

"In your throat, there is a voice box. Think of it lying there—a small box just the size you need to make sounds," Rosie said.

Cinder didn't move. The doll rocked gently above the bridge of her nose, where she had placed it to cover her eyes. Her small stomach moved up and down quickly with her shallow breaths. Her feet pointed inward and her arms were absolutely still by her side.

"When you wake up you are going to speak to me, Cinder. You are going to say, 'Hello Miss Rosetree, I am fine,' " Rosie said. "In just one minute, you are going to sit up on the couch and talk."

The room was suddenly quiet. Lucy sat very still on the picnic basket. Rosie was perched like a stork on the end of her chair, her legs crossed, her chin resting in her hand. And Cinder was still as death.

Rosie had in mind exactly the method she was going to use to take the child out of the trance. In quite a loud voice, she was going to interrupt the silence. "Sit up," she was going to say. *"Talk."*

Instead, without a thought, she leaned forward and took the doll off the child's face.

"No," the mute child said. Her voice was clear and distinct. It filled the silent room with sound. "No rope," she said and sat up, grabbed the doll from Rosie's lap, and stuck it under her yellow sash. And then she marched out of the office of Shrinks, Incorporated, up the driveway, and sat on a tree stump to wait for her nurse.

·10·

First off, Lucy wanted to tell her father that Cinder had talked.

"Not yet," Rosie said.

"Why not? He's been waiting for weeks for her to say something." She took off her scarlet dress and stockings and black high heels and put on gym shorts. "He'll be proud of us."

"All she said was 'No rope,'" Rosie said. "That's not exactly talking."

"Well, what exactly is it?" Lucy asked, disappointed because Rosie had been the one to make the child talk.

"It's not sentences. Now we have to wait for her to tell us the truth."

"What about rope?" Lucy asked.

Rosie shrugged. "I don't know about rope. It could be a clue and it could mean nothing at all. The only thing we know for sure is that she can talk."

Lucy opened the picnic basket and drank all of the Diet Coke without offering any to Rosie.

"We knew that she could talk before," Lucy said. "She simply wouldn't."

Rosie took a handful of Oreos and stuffed them in her pocket.

"Do whatever you like," Rosie said. "I don't care." And she walked out the door of Shrinks, Incorporated. She was not in a very good mood.

Lucy stuffed her clothes in the trunk and took the picnic basket upstairs. In the kitchen, her mother was fixing dinner and listening to classical music on the radio. She didn't hear Lucy slide into a kitchen chair.

"Sometimes I hate Rosie Treeman," Lucy said.

Mrs. Childs sat in a chair across from her.

"You've never been mad at Rosie, darling."

"Well I am now." She put her head down on the table.

"What happened?" Mrs. Childs asked. "Will you tell me?"

"No," Lucy said. "No. No. No." And she picked up Bolivar from the top of the bookcase, where he was biting his toenails, took him into the living room, and lay face down on the couch.

Rosie had everything. She was smart and sweet and pretty and good-tempered and had enough brothers and sisters to fill four ordinary families. Besides, she had a dimple in her left cheek and was good in school. It was not fair that she had been the one to make Cinder talk. Perhaps, Lucy decided, she would fire Rosie from Shrinks, Incorporated, and ask Sally Sweet or Sara Pillsbury or Megan Ruff to take her place. Perhaps she should even quit Shrinks, Incorporated, and open another business.

Lucy was still on the couch when Dr. Childs rushed out of his office, up the driveway, and into the house for dinner, very late. Dinner was drying in the oven.

"I am not eating," Lucy said when she was called.

"Of course you're eating," Dr. Childs said in one of his serious British voices.

"I am sick," Lucy said. "I'm going to bed right away."

Which she did, but she couldn't get to sleep. Her brain spun with waking nightmares. In one of them, she walked along a pale green corridor with black linoleum and no windows, like the one at the University of Virginia Hospital outside Dr. Childs's old office. She held the hand of a large woman in a white nurse's uniform and cape. As they walked, the hand she was holding began to change right before her eyes. Hair grew on the fingers and the grip tightened. When Lucy looked up, the brown-haired head on top of the nurse's uniform was Miss Brill's and she was squeezing Lucy's hand to death. She cried out and Mrs. Childs came to the door.

"Are you all right, darling?" she asked breezily across the dark room. "Maybe I should get you some Coke syrup for your stomach."

"I had a bad dream."

Mrs. Childs sat down on the bed, turned on the light, and rubbed Lucy's head.

"I dreamed about the mute child's nurse, and she was trying to hurt me."

A strange look crossed Mrs. Childs's face.

"I don't find her a pleasant woman."

"You don't think she's dangerous, do you?"

"No, I don't imagine she is. Daddy says she's very competent."

"Well, she gives me the creeps."

Mrs. Childs stayed and rubbed Lucy's head until she was

almost asleep. Then she whispered "Sweet dreams" and closed the door.

The second waking nightmare was not exactly a nightmare but more like the sweet dream Mrs. Childs had wished her daughter.

Behind Dr. Childs's office was a creek, and beside the creek was a willow tree with a rope-and-wood swing that Mrs. Childs's brother had made for Lucy when she was small. The swing went from the bank over the creek to the other side, which was high with reeds and lavender and yellow wildflowers in spring and alive with a concert of crickets in summer. Lucy used to swing for hours when she was a child. Hopping on the swing from the grassy bank, she would stand and pretend that her invented baby sister, Deborah, sat between her legs. Then she would swing from one side to the other, jump off into the wildflowers, take Deborah in her arms, and hide with the child on the soft ground shaded by the overgrowth of reeds. In her waking dream, the child was Cinder and they sat amid the high reeds while Lucy taught her to speak.

"Say Lucy," she said to her.

"Lucy," the child repeated with delight. "Lucy. Lucy. Lucy."

"Tell me what happened that made you stop talking," Lucy asked the child in her dream.

The child shook her head back and forth, put her hands over her eyes.

"I will tell you everything if you promise not to tell," she said to Lucy.

Lucy thought about the dream again and again, but she

simply could not imagine what the mute child would say if she told the truth.

Finally sleeping, she had one more dream, a real and satisfactory one. She was Dr. Forever, sitting at her desk in Shrinks, Incorporated, in her glassless glasses, plaid suit and stockings, and high-heeled shoes with the toes cut out. She was talking on the telephone to St. Elizabeth's Hospital about her patient who lived with a German shepherd and had recently given birth to several German shepherd puppies—and Miss Rosetree, unfortunately, was at home with the chicken pox. There was a knock at the door, and the nurse walked in with a perfectly friendly expression on her face. She sat down in the chair across from Dr. Forever and waited politely for her to finish her conversation. Then she opened a large paper with a great deal of writing in small print and asked her to sign her name at the bottom under hers, which was Madeleine Brill. Lucy signed "Dr. L. Forever" without reading the document.

"Now," she said, shaking her hand, "the mute child is yours. Her parents are dead and she was given to me for safekeeping. I promised the person who gave her to me that I would give her away to the first person who taught her to speak. And that is you."

Rosie was absent from school the following day. Lucy imagined that she had chicken pox, but when she called from the principal's office during third period, Mrs. Treeman said that Rosie had a stomach flu and would be back in school next week.

After lunch there was a note on the bulletin board outside the principal's office for Lucy Childs. "I plan to meet you at four o'clock in front of S.I. Be there without fail. Signed, Miss Rosetree."

The secretary was just coming in from lunch when Lucy got the message.

"Who is Miss Rosetree?" she asked pleasantly. "She sounded very young on the telephone."

"Miss Rosetree," Lucy said without a trace of a smile, "is my great-aunt from Manassas. She has a child's voice." And she went straight to language arts, although she certainly didn't hear a word Miss Grace said about *To Kill a Mockingbird* because she was making up plans.

Rosie Treeman, pale as a ghost, sat on the stoop at the end of the Childs's driveway as Lucy rounded the bend from school.

"I snuck out," she said. "My mother is at exercise class and then she's going to get groceries, and my grandmother is reading the Bible. I can't stay long without being caught. I'm sorry I got mad yesterday."

"Brother, Rosie," Lucy said, full of admiration for her sick friend, who only yesterday she had wished the worst, "you have really changed. You used to be chicken."

"I haven't changed, exactly. But I think we have a responsibility for that child now we've gotten her to talk. We're doctors after all."

"You're right."

"She may have only days to live." Rosie followed Lucy into Shrinks, Incorporated, and flopped on the couch.

"You really think she's in danger?" Lucy asked.

"I know she's in danger," Rosie said. "I dreamed about it. I just don't know how much. Why else do you think I would have come all the way over to the office when I'm throwing up every twelve minutes and feel like dying?"

"Well, what should we do?" Lucy asked.

"I'm depending on you to think of that," Rosie said.

"She may not even come back here, you know. She may be afraid to because you made her talk."

"Maybe." Rosie closed her eyes.

"She may be dead already," Lucy said, caught up in the drama of the moment.

"I doubt that very much," Rosie said.

The child did not knock. She came straight into Shrinks, Incorporated, tiptoeing on cat feet. She was a mess. It looked as if she had been playing in black mud. Her white patent leathers were caked with dried mud. Her pale blue pinafore had muddy prints about the size of her own dirty hands all over the skirt. On her shoulder there were several long, dirty scratches halfway to the elbow. She went over to Miss Rosetree and stood solemnly beside her. Rosie noticed, as she told Lucy later, that the child's pupils were immense, dilated like a scared animal's.

"Hello," Miss Rosetree said quietly. "I'm very glad to see you." She reached out and touched the skirt of Cinder's pinafore.

Then Cinder turned toward Dr. Forever, dipped her head, pulled back her black hair, and revealed a bruise the size of a plum on her neck.

"What happened?" Lucy asked.

But the little girl let her hair fall back, turned away, and walked out the front door of Shrinks, Incorporated. Lucy watched her walk down the pebble drive to wait for Miss Brill.

"So?" Rosie asked. "What do you think?"

Lucy was thinking. "She's trying to tell us something."

"You think someone bruised her neck?" Rosie asked.

"Of course."

"The nurse?"

"Or another child. Or even Mr. Van Dyke," Lucy said. "Unless she bruised her own neck."

"Why would she do that?" Rosie asked, beginning to feel sick again.

"I don't know why. She cut the doll's throat, and I guess that was a message to us. She might bruise her own neck." She went over to her desk, put on her glassless glasses, and sat down in her desk chair. "I've never had to deal with a mute child in all my years as a psychiatrist, Miss Rosetree. I'm doing my best to find out how."

After Lucy went upstairs to get Oreos, Rosie got up and said she had to leave.

"The very sight of Oreos is making me sick."

So Lucy sat alone at her desk and ate the Oreos, one half at a time, and thought about Cinder. She was still sitting at her desk at six-fifteen when the nurse knocked on the door of Shrinks, Incorporated, and said in her tornado voice, "*I am looking for Cinder.*"

"I haven't seen her," Lucy said.

"She was supposed to wait for me on the tree stump at the front of your drive."

"Maybe she's still upstairs with my father," Lucy said.

"I've waited fifteen minutes," the nurse said, and Lucy

heard an edge of panic in her voice. "Your father is never late."

"I'll check," Lucy said. In an emergency, she was permitted to call Dr. Childs on a special telephone number. She ran upstairs to the kitchen. Dr. Childs answered and said that Cinder had of course left an hour before as usual. And then, Lucy remembered the note she and Rosie had left for the nurse. "I'll be right over to speak with the nurse," Dr. Childs said.

Lucy leaned against the kitchen wall. Fortunately her mother was still in her studio, because she needed time to think. She picked up the phone and called Rosie.

"Guess what?" And she told Rosie that Cinder had been missing for an hour and now Dr. Childs and the nurse were going to learn about the forged note.

"I'm glad I'm sick," Rosie said.

"I'm sick too," Lucy said. "Very sick."

"Well, call me when it's all over and tell me what happened."

"I doubt I'll be around when it's all over," Lucy said. "I'll probably be locked in my room for a month."

From the kitchen window Lucy saw a young boy with red hair leave her father's office and walk up the pebble driveway. He stopped and said something to the nurse, who was standing just outside Dr. Childs's office. Then he went on. Shortly afterward, Dr. Childs came out of the office in a hurry and Lucy watched him talk in an agitated way to the nurse.

She imagined the conversation.

"I came at five forty-five and Cinder was gone," the nurse would say.

"She left my office at around four forty-five," Dr. Childs would say.

"Four forty-five?"

"Of course. She always leaves my office at four forty-five."

"But your note?" the nurse would ask.

"What note?"

"The one you wrote to tell me that Cinder would be having double sessions this week."

"I never wrote such a note," Dr. Childs would say.

"Who could have written it then?" the nurse would ask.

She decided at that moment to run away. In minutes, Lucy knew her father would come into the house to look for her. He'd come first to the kitchen, so she would have to leave by the French doors in the dining room across the patio. Which she did. She slid along beside the bushes so Dr. Childs, still in the yard with the nurse, couldn't see her. She crouched down as she dashed behind the rose bushes and the cutting garden. As soon as she was behind her father's office, she ran down the small, now muddy path that wound behind her house to the creek, where the swing was attached to a high willow limb.

The reeds were thick and beige like wheat, and she ducked down, hoping to be camouflaged. The ground was damp, but she sat down anyway, to be hidden while she considered her next move.

The first place her parents would call was the Treemans's, so she couldn't go to Rosie's. But she ought to call Rosie to tell her that she'd left. She'd jump the creek, make her way through the reeds and woods on the other side and go up the hill to the gardens of the houses on Sycamore Street.

Her first grade teacher, Miss Terrell, lived on Sycamore Street, she remembered—on the corner of Sycamore and Main. She could go there for the rest of the afternoon and then make a new decision about the night. Miss Terrell had retired because her brain was failing, but she was very sweet. In fact, her brain was failing so much that she did not remember whether or not Lucy Childs had been a good student in first grade. So she assumed the best and therefore liked Lucy a great deal better than she had when her brain was in good order. Miss Terrell, at least, would be glad to see her, and the Childses would never think of calling her.

She jumped the creek, which at this time of year was wide and high, and made her way up the hill covered with ivy and periwinkle and pachysandra to Sycamore Street. She was just pushing her way through the last group of reeds when she saw the pale blue shimmer of Cinder's pinafore hidden in the beige stalks.

So, she thought, Cinder had run away too.

"Hello," Lucy said quietly.

Cinder put her hands over her eyes.

"I'm so glad you're here," said Lucy. She sat down next to Cinder, and they were hidden by the high reeds. "I'm running away from home."

Cinder put her hands down.

"I've done something awful," Lucy said. "Something I'm not supposed to do, and I'm going to be in a lot of trouble."

Cinder looked at her curiously.

"I mean I would never be beaten or anything," Lucy said. "But my father is going to be quite angry when he finds out what I've done." She rested her head on her knees. "So I've decided to run away."

Cinder picked up the skirt of her pinafore high so it shaded her eyes and Lucy couldn't see the expression on her face, but she could certainly hear what the mute child said.

"Me too," she said distinctly.

Lucy put her hand on Cinder's knee.

"Then we'll have to run away together." She took the child's hand and pulled her up. "I'll take you with me."

Cinder put her doll under her arm and walked with Lucy through the high reeds.

At Main and Sycamore, Lucy called Rosie.

"My father found out about the note so I'm running away from home," she said. "Cinder is with me. I can't talk."

Later, she was very glad she had called Rosie, because, as she told her father, it may have saved her life.

·11·

Instead of visiting Miss Terrell first, Lucy decided, she'd take Cinder to get a root-beer float at Rand's and play a few games of Pac Man in the back of the shop, which she did.

They sat in a high wooden booth, facing each other, Cinder on her knees so she could reach the straw.

And Lucy told her about Shrinks, Incorporated.

"I have a lot of patients," Lucy said. "I have one little girl who hasn't been able to walk ever since she woke up in her crib to find a snake curled on her pillow. All she can do is wriggle on the ground like a snake," Lucy said earnestly. "It's called psychological paralysis, which means it's only in her mind that she can't walk. And I have a little boy named Benjamin exactly your age who is an abused child. Do you know what an abused child is?" Lucy asked.

Cinder shook her head.

"Well," she said, pleased that she had thought to turn the discussion to abused children. "An abused child is beaten or frightened by grown-ups for absolutely no reason." Cinder's eyes were glued to Dr. Forever. "Benjamin's father comes home from work at the shoe factory every afternoon at four. Then he beats Benjamin with a strap and locks him in the closet until dinner. Last week I had his father arrested and he'll be in jail for years, I suppose." She finished all but the ice cream in her root-beer float and ate the ice cream slowly with a long-handled spoon. "You see, my specialty is abused children."

Cinder had not touched her root beer. She sat on her heels, her chubby hands beside her cheeks, just in case she decided to flatten them over her eyes for protection.

"I've saved four children from terrible abuse and seven from a little abuse," Dr. Forever said, carried away by her own success. "Now I'm thinking of adopting one or two to live with me. Especially I'm looking for a girl about your age," she said.

Cinder shook her head.

"Well," Lucy said. "I don't know what you think of her, but I think your nurse is a creep."

Cinder slipped down from her seat, crawled under the table and came up on Lucy's side. She got on the bench beside Lucy and then onto her lap, pressing her small fleshy shoulders into Lucy's bony chest.

"Don't you want your root-beer float?" Lucy asked quietly.

Cinder nodded and pulled the high glass of foamy root beer across the table.

"So," Lucy said, resting her chin on Cinder's shoulder. "Now what is going to happen?"

If Lucy Forever had had eyes behind her head, she would have known exactly what was going to happen. At that very moment, the nurse had walked into the soda shop to look for Cinder and was walking down the aisle of booths.

"Try the shops on Main Street," Dr. Childs had suggested, "and I'll check our back garden and the stream where Lucy sometimes plays." So the nurse had driven to Main Street, parked her car at the south end, gotten out, and walked up the street, checking the shops one after the other. At Rand's she walked down the aisle of booths and stopped when she saw Cinder's black hair over the top of Lucy's shoulder.

Lucy was just getting up to play a game of Pac Man at the back of Rand's when the enormous torso of the nurse blocked her exit.

"Cinder," she whispered in the child's ear. The little girl stiffened to a heavy weight on Lucy. She didn't look at the nurse but scrambled out of the seat, tucked her doll under her arm, gave the nurse her hand, and without a glance backward at Lucy Forever, walked with the nurse toward the door.

"You come, too," the nurse said.

If Lucy had given it a second thought, she wouldn't have gone with Cinder and the nurse for anything—not even to save Cinder, which is why, she decided later, she had followed the nurse down the aisle of Rand's, out the heavy glass door onto Main Street, and up the block to the car.

She sat in the front seat. Cinder climbed in the back.

"I want to go home now," Lucy said quietly.

The nurse did not reply.

"I want to go home now," Lucy said quietly.

The nurse turned the car around and turned right on Rugby Road. In the back seat, Cinder made small muffled cat sounds and the nurse asked her to be quiet, which she did.

"I understand from your father that he had nothing whatsoever to do with a note left on the door of his office which stated that he was increasing Cinder's visits to two hours. Do you know anything about that note?"

"Nothing," Lucy said.

"You are not telling the truth," Miss Brill said in an icy voice.

"I am so."

Lucy expected that her father would be in his office with the red-haired boy when they pulled up in front of the Childs's house but he was not. He was standing at the end of the driveway with his arms folded across his chest, waiting. And Lucy's heart sank. Gone was her chance to run away from home to Miss Terrell's house or even hide in her own room or call Rosie Treeman.

"If you don't stay out of Cinder's business, there is going to be very serious trouble," Miss Brill said. "For you certainly and for Cinder as well."

Lucy didn't reply. She climbed out of the front seat, and her father took her by the wrist as if he expected her to leave instantly.

"I'll see you tomorrow," Dr. Childs said to Miss Brill. "One hour only. I never have two-hour sessions with a child."

In the back seat, Cinder lifted her head and pressed her face against the glass. The look in her round eyes as the car pulled away from the curb was one of terror.

"Did you see her?" Lucy asked her father.

"I saw her," Dr. Childs replied.

He walked in the house behind Lucy and led her upstairs, his hand firm on the small of her back.

"Your mother is at dance class," he said. "I have a patient waiting for me in my office and then one more after him."

Lucy Forever sat down on her bed.

"You are to stay in your room until I come back," he said in the low stern voice that Lucy had never in all of her life defied.

She listened to him walk downstairs, cross the hall into the kitchen, and open the back door. Then she crawled under the covers, but every time she closed her eyes, all she could see was the terrified look of the mute child.

Finally she tiptoed across the hall into her parents' room and called Miss Rosetree.

"Rosie is sick," her mother said.

"This is an emergency," Lucy said.

"You have too many emergencies for a normal girl, Lucy Childs," Mrs. Treeman said, but she let Rosie come to the phone nevertheless.

Lucy told her everything.

"You're going to have to go rescue her," Rosie said. She lowered her voice to a whisper. "Something awful is going on in that home."

"I wish you could come with me."

"Me too," Rosie said. "But I can't."

∘ 12 ∘

The grandfather clock in the hall struck seven o'clock. Outside it was almost dusk, the color of oatmeal— and in minutes Mrs. Childs would drive the yellow Peugeot into the driveway and hop out in her leotards with a bag of groceries.

Lucy ran down the front steps, leapt over Bolivar, who lay on his back on the hall rug, and rushed out the side door in the dining room to the shed, where she got her bicycle. Her father, had he been looking out the window of his office, would have seen her ride her bike across the grass and down the driveway. Her mother had just turned onto Rugby Road as Lucy raced across it and continued behind the Olssons's house, through the Tayers's side yard, to Arch Street. Then she rode down Arch Street to University Avenue and headed toward Cedar Tree Lane. At Eckart Drugs, she decided to call Rosie once more.

"Whatever you do, don't tell my parents where I am," she made Rosie promise. "As soon as they know I'm missing, they'll call you for sure."

Rosie promised.

"Unless of course something terrible happens to me," Lucy reconsidered.

"How will I know that?" Rosie asked.

"I suppose if I disappear," Lucy said, "and am still gone by tomorrow morning."

"It's almost dark now," Rosie said ominously.

Lucy could see that very well. She hopped back on her bike and rode as fast as she could past the outskirts of Charlottesville to Cedar Tree Lane. By the time she arrived at the Albemarle County Home for Children and locked her bike to a streetlight post, it was dusk.

Her plan was to go straight up to the front door, ring the doorbell, and ask to speak to Miss Brill.

"I have come to speak to you," she intended to say as Miss Brill escorted her to her office. "I have come to apologize for the invasion of privacy." Invasion of privacy was her father's favorite expression. She imagined that Miss Brill would give her a lecture and then dismiss her, but at least Lucy would have a chance to look around the home and perhaps even to see Cinder. She might discover a clue.

However, just as she walked up the cement path, there was a strange wail, the sound made by a small animal who has been injured, or a child. The sound seemed to come from the second-story window and go on and on and on. As Lucy looked up, she could see Miss Brill staring down at her. Frightened, she ducked under a large rhododendron bush lining the path and waited.

If Miss Brill had not been looking out the window as Lucy walked up the path to the Albemarle Home for Children, Lucy would have rushed back to her bicycle and ridden home just in time for Dr. Childs to finish with his last patient for the day. But the fact was Miss Brill did see Lucy before the screaming even began and walked down the stairs to the front door after Billy bit Sammy in the shoulder so hard that Sammy screamed at the top of his lungs, which was the wail Lucy heard. This did not stop Miss Brill, who was accustomed to the screams of children and, besides, Billy was always biting someone. She opened the front door and went out on the porch. Lucy, under the rhododendron bush, heard her but did not move. She could see Miss Brill in the porch light pacing back and forth, looking into the darkness of the yard. Then she went inside, turned off the porch light, and the yard was black.

For what seemed to be a long time, Lucy lay there. The screaming stopped as abruptly as it had started. In the upstairs window, she could barely see a child—a girl with braids, framed in light. In the far distance, she heard a piano playing. Perhaps Mr. Van Dyke was giving Cinder her lesson. Still she waited.

Eventually the porch light went on again and Lucy saw Mr. Van Dyke come out in his trench coat with Cinder. The child's head was down, and although the piano teacher seemed to be speaking to her, she did not respond. Then Miss Brill came up behind Cinder, put her hands on Cinder's shoulders, and drew her back inside.

Mr. Van Dyke stood on the top step of the porch and looked into the dark yard.

Certainly Miss Brill had told him Lucy was hiding there. He went from one end of the steps to the other, staring out; he looked like a crane, with his head foolishly stretched toward the horizon. Then, satisfied not to have seen Lucy Forever, he bounded down the steps, jumped into his car parked in the driveway of the home, and drove toward Charlottesville.

Only after he was gone did Lucy crawl out from under the rhododendron bush. She made her way to the house, pausing once at a large cement urn cracked in the middle with an evergreen tree planted in it. She certainly did not want Miss Brill to catch her in the middle of the yard, but she didn't know what to do now that it was too dark to ride home. She could, of course, knock on the front door and apologize to Miss Brill, as she had planned to do initially, and then ask to call her mother to pick her up. Or she could go quickly up the front steps of the Home for Children, hide out next to the long front window, and spy. Which is what she decided to do first.

The windows on either side of the front door were long, floor to ceiling, and as wide as the door. Lucy could see everything. The wide stairs, the long hall where a small boy sat on the floor in pajama tops and diapers with a stuffed bear upside down in his lap. The small boy stared out through the window where Lucy was, although certainly he could not see her because of the darkness. She was struck by his attention to nothing. He stared straight ahead as though the air were full of people. Then she heard the voice of a woman upstairs—probably Miss Brill.

"Thomas," the woman called. "Thomas, come here."

If the boy was Thomas, he did not seem to recognize his name. He did not move.

Then Miss Brill clattered to the landing with a baby under one arm, walked down the steps, and stopped where the child was sitting.

"Thomas," she said evenly. And she took a handful of the child's black hair and shook him and shook him like a mop. "Follow me upstairs," she said.

But Thomas simply sat there as though nothing had interrupted his thoughts and stared into the darkness.

"Stupid boy," she said. And then, without provocation, the enormous woman kicked Thomas in the back and he toppled over.

Even after Miss Brill had disappeared upstairs, he remained folded in half on the landing, and for a moment Lucy was afraid he was dead.

Shortly, however, Miss Brill returned without the baby under her arm, took hold of the boy's hair in her thick hand, and dragged him upstairs. He did not even cry.

But Lucy Forever, weak from fear of what she had witnessed, was afraid she might be sick. Surely she had come upon more real trouble than even Dr. Forever, with her interest in danger, wished to see.

At eight o'clock, Dr. Childs called Rosie Treeman. He was sitting in the kitchen with Mrs. Childs. Mrs. Childs was crying and dinner was in the oven drying to dust. Darkness had come early, with promise of a storm, and the Childses were frantic. Although they hoped that Lucy was hiding because of the forged note and would have the courage to return by dinner, Mrs. Childs had called all of Lucy's friends, including Rosie.

No one had seen Lucy except Sally Perkins, who said she

saw Lucy having a root-beer float with a little girl at Rand's.

Rosie told Dr. Childs she did not know about Lucy.

"She hasn't called me," Rosie lied and said three Hail Marys, begging forgiveness for disobedience and dishonesty.

"Perhaps Rosie is not telling the truth," Dr. Childs said to Mrs. Childs.

"Rosie?" Mrs. Childs exclaimed. "Rosie always tells the truth."

"Perhaps," Dr. Childs said, "but I think I ought to let her mother know what has been going on, nevertheless." So he called Mrs. Treeman and told her the whole situation, including the forged note.

Mrs. Treeman was very upset.

"As soon as this situation is resolved, you are not allowed to participate in Shrinks, Incorporated, again," she said to Rosie.

Rosie didn't reply. She knew her mother well enough to know that any conversation would make matters worse.

"I'm not pleased with your friendship with Lucy Childs now that you've gotten older. She has too many ideas," Mrs. Treeman said.

"She's very sensible and I'm sure she's fine," Rosie said, but she was very worried about Dr. Forever now that a storm was coming and it was night.

Lucy leaned against the wall next to the long front window and thought. She was afraid. She could feel a storm moving in from the Blue Ridge Mountains. The air was suddenly much colder and a wind had picked up, tearing at the tops of the trees. It was going to rain. She no longer wanted to apologize to Miss Brill or see the inside of the Albemarle Home for Children. In fact, even the thought of Miss Brill made her head ache as if her own hair had been pulled like Thomas's. She certainly would like to see Cinder to be sure she was all right, but most of all she wanted to go home to her own bed, to her sweet quiet mother, even to her father's bad humor.

The rain started in a torrent, flying in sheets out of the sky, sailing between the pillars onto the porch until Lucy was soaked through her sweater and blue jeans and cold to the bone. She did not see Cinder come down the long flight of stairs in her blue nightgown, did not hear her walk across the hall and press her nose against the window where Lucy stood just to the left, hidden from view. But when Lucy looked up, there was Cinder, her eyes brimming with sadness.

Lucy knelt next to the window and pressed her face against the glass even with Cinder's. She was so pleased to see the child that she did not see Miss Brill start down the stairs, stop, transfixed by the sight of Lucy Forever in the glass, then quietly turn around and go upstairs.

But Cinder heard the nurse. She did not look around but instead, like an automated doll, she walked backward away from the window. Lucy motioned to her to come back, but Cinder simply shook her head and kept walking slowly backward. At the steps, she turned around and walked up the stairs slowly, without looking at Lucy, and disappeared.

Then, suddenly, the porch was flooded with light. Lucy

leaned flat against the wall of the house as she had seen criminals in movies do, her back and arms paper flat, her head turned to the side, her stomach pulled in so she could not be seen. Her heart pounded furiously. In seconds, Miss Brill was going to open the front door and take hold of her, she was sure.

Which is exactly what happened. Just as Lucy decided to jump off the side of the porch and run into the darkness of the yard, Miss Brill opened the front door, grabbed her arm, put her hand over Lucy's mouth, twisted her arm behind her back so it bent like a pretzel, lifted her off the ground, and carried her inside.

Without effort, she carried Lucy through the hall, the dining room, and down the corridor that led to the kitchen, turning off the lights with her elbow as she walked, in order not to let go her hold on Lucy's mouth. The last part of the journey was in darkness. Lucy was put in a small room that smelled thickly of Lysol and pine oil. She heard Miss Brill lock the door from the outside.

"I'm putting the children to bed and then I'll be back to tend to you," Miss Brill said.

Lucy groped around the small room, which was a little larger than she was. It had shelves filled with cleaning supplies and rags and sponges—a utility closet. She crawled into a small corner of the room under a shelf.

Perhaps, she thought, Miss Brill had in mind to kill her. She could easily strangle Lucy in a flash and no one would know. She could put the children to bed, come down to the kitchen, strangle Lucy Forever, put her in a green garbage bag, and toss her in the trash can. There would be no evidence whatsoever.

Except, Lucy thought to herself, Cinder. Cinder had seen her. If she were willing to talk, Cinder could tell Dr. Childs that his daughter was dead in a garbage bag.

There was a small cry in the room above the utility closet and then the heavy clatter of Miss Brill's black, square-heeled shoes on the stairs. The light went on in the kitchen and slid under the door to the utility closet. Lucy was terrified. She could not stop shaking.

At nine o'clock Rosie Treeman went to bed. She knelt down and said her prayers, automatically thinking all along of Lucy Forever in terrible trouble. She climbed into her bed, asked her older sister to turn down the radio and her younger sister to turn off the light, and closed her eyes. She did not, of course, fall asleep. She was much too stirred up for sleeping, so she heard the telephone ring clear as a bell at nine-thirty. Then she heard her mother walk down the corridor toward her bedroom.

"Rosemary," Mrs. Treeman said. "The police are coming with Dr. Childs to see you. Get up and *dress*," she said.

Rosie got up. She put on her navy blue skirt and white blouse, which she wore only to Mass and family dinners. She wanted the police to know immediately by her dress that she was a good Catholic girl. She brushed her hair and her teeth and put tiny gold studs in her pierced ears. Then she went downstairs, where her grandmother sat reading the Bible and her mother sat watching television and sewing on buttons and her father sat in an overstuffed arm chair lacing his high-top work shoes.

"Blessed are the meek, for they shall inherit the earth," her grandmother said, quoting her favorite lines. "I understand you are in trouble, Rosemary, and you must be humble. Humble children who have been bad do not get in trouble, you know."

"I am humble," Rosie said and sat down on the high-backed chair beside her grandmother.

"Don't speak back to your grandmother," Mrs. Treeman said.

"She did not speak back," her grandmother said. "She spoke the truth. She is a good and humble girl."

"The police will not be interested in her humility, Mother," her father said. He kissed his wife and his mother goodbye.

"Tell the truth," he said to Rosie severely. "The police are only interested in the truth. Call me if there is an emergency," he said to his wife.

"Is this an emergency?" Rosie's grandmother asked.

The doorbell rang. Mrs. Treeman turned off the television.

"Of course it's an emergency," she said crossly.

Rosie sat very still and waited. There were two policemen, one in uniform and another in an ordinary business suit. One sat on the couch where Mrs. Treeman had been sitting and the other sat in the chair where Mr. Treeman had been tying his shoes. Dr. Childs came in as well and stood next to the fireplace with his arm on the mantle, his hand on a statue of the Blessed Mother. He was the color of chalk.

Rosie knew from the start that she would have to tell the truth. This was an emergency. There was no choice. She did not even wait to be asked.

"Lucy called me and said she was on her way to the Albemarle Home for Children, where one of Dr. Childs's patients lives." She folded her hands neatly in her lap. "I'm sorry I lied to you," she said to Dr. Childs.

"You lied," Mrs. Treeman said. "There is no sorry for lying."

"No kin of mine has ever lied," Rosie's grandmother said with confidence and opened the Bible again.

"I called the home," Dr. Childs said. "Miss Brill, the nurse in charge, said she had not seen Lucy but that she'd check around the grounds as soon as the storm has let up."

"Maybe Lucy got caught in the rain and stopped somewhere," Mrs. Treeman said.

"Maybe she was kidnapped," Rosie's grandmother said ominously. "Or hit by a car or a truck. Terrible things can happen to children who don't obey their parents." She looked sadly at Rosie.

"Maybe the nurse was lying to you," Rosie said to Dr. Childs.

"That, of course, is possible," Dr. Childs said. He picked up the telephone and called Mrs. Childs, who had stayed at home just in case Lucy called. There was no news from Mrs. Childs. Then he called Miss Brill again.

Miss Brill answered the telephone in the kitchen on the second ring. She had just finished putting the children to bed and turned on the light to check on Lucy Forever locked in the closet.

"I have just finished with the children," Miss Brill said. "I'll go outside with my flashlight and check the yard right now, although I certainly don't understand why she would wish to come here."

"To apologize to you about the forged note," Dr. Childs said.

"Then she should have come straight up to the front door and apologized like a normal little girl," she said crossly.

"Of course she should have," Dr. Childs agreed.

"I'll call you back shortly," Miss Brill said.

"Never mind," Dr. Childs said. "I have the police with me, and I think we'll come over and take a look ourselves."

Miss Brill hung up the telephone.

Lucy heard her walk across the floor away from her, although she had not heard the conversation with Dr. Childs. Then the light in the kitchen went out and the key turned in the closet lock. When the door opened, Miss Brill was shining a flashlight in Lucy's face. Lucy hid her face in her knees.

"Get up," Miss Brill said quietly.

Lucy got up, leaning against the wall as far away from Miss Brill as she could get.

"Come out here," Miss Brill said, and Lucy did.

"Are you going to hurt me?" Lucy asked.

"Put your hands together behind your back."

But Lucy didn't. She turned around and began to run out of the kitchen, screaming in a long thin voice, but Miss Brill was very fast and grabbed her, stuffed a dish towel in her mouth, bound her hands behind her back, and tied her up.

"Of course I'm going to hurt you," Miss Brill said hot in her ear, and at that moment the light in the kitchen went on and Cinder stood in the doorway in her pale blue flowered nightgown.

Lucy was the first to see her.

"No," Cinder said in a clear voice.

"See," Miss Brill said through her teeth. "You can speak. Of course you can speak. Now go to bed immediately." She lifted Lucy under her arm like a rug.

"No," Cinder said. "I won't go to bed."

So with her free arm, Miss Brill hit the child on the head, and Cinder fell over like a rag doll in the corner of the kitchen. Miss Brill turned out the light.

"You see," Miss Brill said in Lucy's ear, "I could kill you."

·13·

Rosie rode in the police car with Dr. Childs, the detective, and the chief of police. They drove slowly down University Avenue to Route 36, just in case Lucy Forever might be walking along the road or riding her bike on the slick streets. As they turned into Cedar Tree Lane, they passed a car traveling too fast for a rainy night, and Rosie turned around to look out the back window because the car seemed familiar. But it had disappeared, and she didn't mention anything to Dr. Childs.

They pulled up in front of the Albemarle County Home for Children and got out. The light on the front porch was on and they rang the doorbell. No one answered. They waited and rang again. A small boy in diapers and pajama tops appeared at the landing of the stairs and looked out, but he did not answer the door.

"I'm certain she's here," Dr. Childs said. "I spoke with her."

He went over to the side of the porch and looked in the driveway.

"Doesn't she have a station wagon?" he asked Rosie.

Rosie nodded.

"Well, there is no car in the driveway." He went around to the side of the house and then back on the porch again. "The car is gone," he said.

"I think I saw it," Rosie said quietly.

"You saw it? Where?"

"On this street going the other way," Rosie said.

"Why didn't you tell me?"

"I thought I saw it. I could have been wrong."

The policeman wanted to check inside first.

"Can I try the door?" Dr. Childs asked.

"Try it," the policeman said.

Dr. Childs turned the knob and the door opened easily. They walked into a large hall and followed the corridor to the kitchen, which was dark.

Everything in the kitchen seemed in order when the policeman turned on the light. The door to the utility closet was open, however, and some floor wax had spilled in a small stream across the linoleum to the other side of the room. Right next to the doorway was a small red circle about the size of a tennis ball.

He leaned down and took a careful look.

"Blood," he said quietly.

White-faced with worry, Dr. Childs led the way upstairs. There were eleven rooms with two children to a room. He went from room to room turning on the lights. The sleeping children stirred when the light went on, but they did not wake up. In the last room were three beds—two held little girls with pale yellow hair whose heads peeked out of the blankets. The third bed had been slept in but was empty. The pillow showed a hollow where a child's head had been, the covers were thrown back. Dr. Childs checked the bed, and there was the doll Rosie had given Cinder, face down under the pillow.

Dr. Childs stood up and folded his hands tightly together to keep from shaking.

"I suppose it is possible that Miss Brill has taken Cinder and Lucy as well."

He followed the policeman and detective down the corridor beyond the children's rooms.

Miss Brill's room was in chaos. The closet door was open and all the clothes were gone. Hangers had been thrown all over the floor and the bed. The dresser drawers were open and empty. The tops of tables were cleared, and on the bed in a pile of nurses uniforms were the black tack-heeled shoes she always wore.

"She's left." Dr. Childs sat weakly on the bed.

"She certainly seems to have," the policeman said.

"Do you think she has Lucy?" Rosie asked. Dr. Childs did not reply.

"I should have told you," Rosie said. "I should never have lied."

"Yes, you should have told me," Dr. Childs said. "But a number of things that should have been done were not. I should have checked into Miss Brill more carefully."

They did not hear the small bare feet of Thomas pad down the hallway. The policeman was checking the drawers and closets, opening the side drawers of the bedside table. Dr. Childs was talking softly to Rosie, so Thomas was in the room before anybody noticed him. He stood in the middle of the bedroom with his small hands behind his back.

"Cinder is dead," he said solemnly. "I saw."

"How did she die?" Dr. Childs asked quietly.

"Miss Brill."

"You saw that?"

Thomas shook his head. "I saw her carry Cinder dead to her car. I was looking out the window."

"You know she's dead?"

Thomas hesitated. "I think."

Dr. Childs was too shaken to move. The detective helped him up.

"Perhaps your daughter is not with Miss Brill," he said. He turned to Thomas. "Did you see another girl?"

Thomas shook his head.

"Only Cinder dead and Miss Brill in her car," Thomas said.

The detective stayed at the home, which was unsupervised without Miss Brill. The policeman drove Dr. Childs and Rosie home, although both of them were too agitated to sleep. An alarm went out to the police in several states to be on the lookout for Miss Brill's station wagon. The police and Dr. Childs assumed that she had Cinder—maybe dead, maybe not—with her, and Lucy Childs.

Rosie lay in her bed and listened to her sisters' gentle breathing, unable to settle down herself. Twice in the middle of the night, her mother came in to check on her, imagining perhaps that Rosie too might run away from home. Each time, Rosie pretended to be sleeping. At six, the sky was turning pink and Rosie crept out of bed, slipped down the stairs to the telephone in the kitchen, and called the Childses.

Dr. Childs answered on the first ring.

"Is there any news?" Rosie asked.

"Just now the police called," Dr. Childs said, and his voice sounded as old as the earth. "They have picked up Miss Brill in Tennessee."

"And Lucy?"

"Miss Brill was traveling alone."

He was afraid that Lucy was dead. Rosie could tell by the heavy sound of resignation in his voice.

"If you can pick me up, we should go to the home," Rosie said. "Maybe Lucy is there. In fact," she said, although she did not believe it at all, "I *know* she's there."

They drove to Cedar Tree Lane just as the sun peered over the horizon.

"We have a lot of information from the police," Dr. Childs said to Rosie. "Miss Brill has a record of child abuse."

"Lucy guessed that," Rosie said.

"She was a nurse in a pediatric hospital in Kentucky and was fired for beating a child badly. And then she got a job at an orphanage in Philadelphia, where she burned a child's back with an iron. Her name is not Miss Brill at all. She made up a record of jobs and a whole new identity when she came to Charlottesville."

"Do you think she's the one who slit Cinder's throat?"

"I don't know," Dr. Childs said. "I do know that the social worker who visited the home for children had suspicions but never told the police and that Mr. Van Dyke once witnessed her beating a little boy called Thomas and was paid to keep quiet."

"Did she say anything to the police about Lucy when she was caught?"

"Nothing. She won't talk."

They pulled into the driveway of the home and got out. The early morning was dew-damp and chilly, but the sun was beginning to burn through.

Rosie ran ahead, her heart beating in her throat. She dashed by the policeman sitting on the bottom step, raced upstairs past Thomas, who peered forlornly between the railings, down the upstairs corridor, running from room to room, flinging open the closet doors, looking under the beds, in the linen closets, in the dark attic.

"Lucy," she called frantically. "Lucy, please answer."

She met Dr. Childs at the top of the stairs.

"They are bringing Miss Brill back here," he said.

"Maybe she'll tell us where they are." Rosie ran downstairs, through the kitchen, checking the pantry and broom closet. She opened the door to the basement and stepped down slowly so her eyes could adjust to darkness. Then she heard a sound—it could have been the sound of an animal, perhaps a rat, she thought. In front of her was a large freezer, some packing boxes, an ironing board, a sled, and a door. The sound came from behind the door.

"Lucy," she called.

The sound came again, muffled like the sound of a human voice, not the scuttle of rodents.

"Lucy," she called again and flung open the door. Lucy Forever, her arms and legs bound in ropes, her mouth gagged, tumbled out the door.

Miss Brill had tied her arms and legs together, stuffed an old linen napkin in her mouth, dragged her down the basement steps, and pushed her into the closet where Rosie found her. Then Miss Brill had rushed upstairs, picked up Cinder, and left.

Even Mrs. Treeman agreed to let Rosie stay home from school. All morning Rosie and Lucy Forever lay around the office of Shrinks, Incorporated, and let Mrs. Childs bring them apple juice and cookies and sliced oranges and strawberries and egg salad sandwiches cut in tiny squares while they talked about Cinder in hushed voices.

The police, who had a search party looking in several counties of Virginia, assumed that Cinder was dead and that Miss Brill had hidden her body either at the home or someplace along the route between Charlottesville and Tennessee.

Lucy, however, did not believe Cinder was dead. She believed the child was hiding someplace in the home and would not come out until she felt safe from the dreadful nurse.

"What about the blood we found on the floor of the kitchen?" Rosie asked.

"It's Cinder's blood. Miss Brill hit her as she was leaving the kitchen with me last night, but that doesn't mean she has to die just because she bled."

Rosie shrugged. "Maybe not," she agreed. "Maybe we should go look for her ourselves, if your mother would let us out of her sight for a minute."

"She won't, I'm sure. But I can ask her to take us to the home."

So the next time Mrs. Childs came downstairs to Shrinks, Incorporated, with a dish of oatmeal cookies hot from the oven and two glasses of cold milk, Lucy asked. Mrs. Childs agreed without any hesitation. She took off her smock and ballet shoes and got the keys to the yellow Peugeot.

"She was heartbroken about me," Lucy said. "I bet she'd do absolutely anything I asked."

"Then you'd better ask for everything you might ever want right now," Rosie said.

Which was exactly Lucy's thinking.

"If by any chance Cinder is alive," Lucy said to her mother, "I think we should consider adopting her."

"Of course, darling," Mrs. Childs said softly. "Of course we'll do that."

Mrs. Childs backed slowly out of the driveway and they started down Rugby Road, out University Avenue to Cedar Tree Lane. Just as the car turned onto Cedar Tree Lane, Lucy saw a child way in the distance walking down the middle of the road.

"Look," Mrs. Childs said, "there's a child who's going to be hurt if she doesn't get out of the street."

As they drove closer, the child walked straight toward them.

"It's as if she wants to be hit," Mrs. Childs said, slowing down.

And then Lucy knew.

"Rosie," she said, "look."

"Mother," Lucy said, "stop the car right here." And she jumped out, ran toward Cinder, and lifted her in her arms.

·14·

On Monday afternoon Miss Rosetree, dressed in paisley, her hair in its usual bun, sat at her desk at Shrinks, Incorporated, and talked on the telephone to a woman whose cat peed on the living room couch whenever it rained.

"This is not a serious problem," Miss Rosetree said matter-of-factly. "We have dealt with a great many perfectly normal cats who do that. If you'd like an appointment, I'll give you my assistant." She handed the telephone to Cinder, who was dressed in Mrs. Childs's red taffeta evening dress, tied around the waist with a red bandanna so it was short enough. She had on dyed lavender high-heeled shoes and a hat.

"Hello," Cinder said into the telephone. And then she looked at Miss Rosetree. She was confused. "I don't know how to play this game yet."

"It's very easy," Miss Rosetree said and took Cinder on her lap. "All you do is pretend to be a doctor and believe you are a good one. And that's that. You can be anything you wish to be."

Cinder looked at Miss Rosetree.

"Anything?" she asked.

"Within reason," Rosie said.

"Well," Cinder said. "I'd like to be Dr. Forever's baby sister."

Upstairs, Dr. Forever, in school clothes, talked to the detective and the chief of police. She told them everything she knew from the start, including the detailed account Cinder had given her that morning.

"What about her throat?" Dr. Childs asked. "Did she tell you about her throat?"

"Miss Brill cut her throat, but not exactly on purpose. She was cutting a piece of rope to tie Cinder in bed at night since she had threatened to run away, and Cinder came into the kitchen. Apparently Miss Brill flung out her hand with the knife in it and said 'Go away,' and the knife accidentally cut Cinder's throat. Then she told Cinder if she ever told anyone, especially the social worker, how her throat was cut, Miss Brill would strangle her with the rope."

"And so she decided not to talk," Dr. Childs said.

"Maybe she decided and maybe she simply couldn't," Lucy said. "But she is certainly talking now."

After the detectives and the chief of police had left and the *Charlottesville Daily Progress* reporters had come to take a picture of Lucy and Cinder and Rosie to go with the story on the front page—CHILD PSYCHIATRISTS' SUCCESS STORY—Rosie and Cinder had gone back downstairs to the basement to play Shrinks. The Childses sat in the kitchen at the table in the light and warmth of the afternoon sun.

"So what will happen to the child?" Mrs. Childs said to

Dr. Childs. He did not answer at once but stared out the window.

"Perhaps," Mrs. Childs said, "we should take her."

Dr. Childs was thoughtful. He folded his hands, looked across the table at his wife. "Perhaps we should," he said.

Lucy couldn't believe her ears. She picked up Bolivar, rushed up the stairs to her bedroom, put on a blue silk shirt and wool skirt, did her hair in a floppy bun, put on her glassless glasses, put Bolivar under her arm, and went downstairs to the kitchen, where she filled her pockets full of Oreos. Her parents were still at the kitchen table.

"So," she said, "I'm off to work. I'll be up for dinner."

Downstairs, she went straight to her desk and picked up the telephone.

"Dr. Forever speaking," she said. "Just a moment, please. Cinder?" she said. "Telephone for you."

"I can't talk," Cinder said.

"You have to," Dr. Forever said. "There's a child on the phone who needs your help."

Cinder climbed up on Lucy's lap and took the phone and listened. She listened intently for a long time. Then she said, "Just a minute, please. You can speak to Dr. Forever. She's the best doctor in the world." And she opened her Oreo and gave Lucy Forever the half with the icing.

SUSAN SHREVE has produced an impressive range of fiction, from books for teens to several novels for adults. Her work for younger children includes *Lily and the Runaway Baby* and *The Flunking of Joshua T. Bates*.

A graduate of the University of Pennsylvania and recipient of a Guggenheim Fellowship, Ms. Shreve is currently an associate professor of English at George Mason University. She lives with her husband, a literary agent, in Washington, D.C.